I0571726

The Four Seasons Murders
A Morgan Crew Short Mystery Compilation

The Four Seasons Murders

A Morgan Crew Short Mystery Compilation

ARTHUR A. LEE

LEEWARD PUBLISHERS, LLC
Winter Garden, Florida

The Four Seasons Murders
A Morgan Crew Short Story Compilation

Arthur Lee

This is a work of fiction. Names, characters, places and incidents are either the product of the author's imagination or are used fictionally, and resemblance to actual persons living or dead, business establishments, events or locales is entirely coincidental.

Copyright © 2013 by Arthur Lee & Leeward Publishers, LLC

All rights reserved. This book, in whole and in part, is the property of the author. No part of this book may be reproduced or transmitted in any form or by any means, graphic, electronic, or mechanical, including but not limited to photocopying, recording, taping, or by any information storage retrieval system, without the permission in writing from the author.

ISBN: 978-0615839387

In accordance with the U.S. Copyright Act of 1976, the scanning, uploading, and electronic sharing of any part of the book without the permission of the publisher constitute unlawful piracy and theft of the author's intellectual property. If you would like to use material from the book (other than for review purposes), prior written permission must be obtained by contacting the publisher at

Silver Cat Press
An Imprint of Leeward Publishers, LLC

Other Books by the Author

The Morgan Crew Mystery Series

A Storm In From The Sea
The Las Vegas Murders
A Deadly London Fog
The Hawaiian Sunset Murders
The Spy Who Would Not Speak
The West Texas Murders

The Four Seasons Murders

A Morgan Crew Short Story Compilation

By

Arthur A. Lee

Contents

WINTER KILL

THE HOOK

"As I recall, this was another one of your ideas," Sandy said, just a little bit of jailhouse humor lilting her words.

We had awoken to the soft buzzing of the alarm clock on the bedside table. The red numbers on the face indicated it was half past nine in the AM, but the room was dark. I slid out of bed and into my beat-up old leather slippers; the rabbit fur flattened and all but non-existent after all these years. I walked across the room, shuffling my feet across the expensive carpet so the old, stretched-out slippers wouldn't fall off my feet. Still half asleep, I had forgotten that the old slippers were the only clothing I was wearing. Sandy's wolf whistle reminded me of the fact.

Reaching the big window, I pulled the heavy green brocade drapery aside and looked out. It was snowing hard. The world was a cold, still, steel gray. I couldn't see more than two feet past the glass of the window.

"Guess what, Sandy dear?" I said.

"Morgan, my dear," she said as she pulled the down comforter up around her. "Nothing you could tell me would surprise me. Being married to you is one big surprise after

1

another. But I do love it!"

I had met Sandy D'Angelo in San Marcos, California, my hometown. Death and danger had surrounded our meeting but love had kept us together. Sandy had never known wealth and privilege before, but she had not become overwhelmed with it now that she had become part of it. The huge Crew family fortune was not something she wore as lavish pride. Every day was new to her and she drank in the advantages of my wealth in small, gentle sips so it would not intoxicate her. She enjoyed it but inside she was too real, too down-to-earth to allow all the money to go to her head.

And in the short time we have been together, the cloak of danger has followed us like a black cloud always on the horizon, always threatening, always dark and foreboding. We had overcome a vast criminal organization in San Marcos; we had saved my worthless cousin and a high-rollers' casino (which I own, by the way) in Las Vegas, where I had come very close to losing Sandy to the vengeance of a Mafia prince; and we had survived and won a war against an insane and blood thirsty criminal in London.

It seems my life has been designed to be put at risk to help other people. And Sandy has chosen to live this life of risk with me. The love we share, I am certain, is stronger than any jeopardy we could be thrown into.

"Well, surprise, surprise," I said as I let the drapery slip from my fingers. "We're not going home today, my love."

"What do you mean? We have a train to catch this afternoon," she said in a sexy, sleepy voice.

"No trains, dear. And no cars either. I think we're snowed in."

"What!" she shouted and tossed the thick comforter away. She jumped from the bed and ran to the window, forgetting that she, too, slept in the buff. Not that I was going to complain, of course. At the window she pulled the drapery aside and stared out at the thick blanket of snow two floors below and the big, heavy flakes falling from a never ending black sky. "Oh, damn!" she exclaimed. "I have the painters coming in tomorrow."

Our house in the hills of San Marcos, overlooking the harbor, had been my home for years before meeting Sandy. I could not stay in the old mansion, with its eight bedrooms, that my parents and their parents before them had lived in. I had my home built to my specifications, with lots of glass and enough room to be comfortable but not extravagant. But it was dark and masculine in a heavy-handed way. Sandy was changing all that, little by little.

The painters would have to wait, it seemed. This trip to a valley in the Montana Mountains had been my idea. The Crew family owns The Sun River Resort and Guest Ranch. The family hosts a celebrity golf tournament every August at the Resort. I had wanted to attend this year's October planning session for next year's event. I hadn't expected this much snow however. That was when Sandy said, "As I recall, this was another one of your ideas."

We dressed quickly and ran downstairs to the front desk. The Resort was closed for the season and only a small kitchen staff stayed on for the meeting, but a radio at the desk told us that I was right again. The roads were all closed and the forecast was foreboding. But I knew that the wine cellar and the liquor bar were well stocked. I also had made sure that there was a good supply of Wild Turkey bourbon on hand. What a relief; if I'm going to be snowed in for God knows how long, I need my two or three Wild Turkeys a day.

So, we went back to our room, shared a shower, and wound up in bed again. We finally went back downstairs just past eleven to find my fellow committee members and a couple of late season guests of the resort in the main dining room, sitting at a large table in front of a roaring fire set in the big stone hearth. They were drinking coffee and complaining loudly of being stranded.

The committee consisted of Roger Townsend of

Premier National Bank who brought along Bridgett, his third wife. It seems each of Roger's wives, in turn, gets younger than the one before.

Lyle Porter was there; he had appointed himself to take over the committee spot held by his father, who had recently passed away. Lyle at the time was thirty-eight years old and unmarried. The rumors of his being homosexual were compounded by the fact that, although there were stories of him seducing wives of friends, there were other stories of him seducing a few of the husbands and sons of those wives, too.

Terry Adams, a former PGA player who had quit the tour and started a golf course design company (financed by a few million dollars from a Crew family bank) rounded out the committee I chaired. His wife, Marlene, was there and until I met Sandy I had never known a finer, gentler, kinder, smarter woman in my whole life. Her health had been waning in recent years; she was not as active as she once was, but the bright smile seldom left her face.

There was another couple, not with the committee, in the dining room, having traveled into the valley in an RV two evenings ago. They said they had taken a wrong turn and found themselves at the resort. They had arrived sometime after 10 PM and I agreed that they should stay the night rather than drive into the early morning to get back to the highway.

They said the resort looked so nice they wanted to stay a day or two, which I had agreed to as long as they pay for their food and booze. They had not expected to be snowed in so early in the year as they drove east out of the Rockies.

Sandy and I joined the group and were thankful for the great coffee the resort sported. Knowing it was almost lunchtime, we did not mention breakfast.

"Damn it, Morgan!" Roger shouted as he saw me walk into the room. "I told you we should have this damn meeting in Chicago!"

"Rog, ol' buddy," I said as Sandy and I sat at a table with our coffee. "You want the planning committee to meet in Chicago every year. Could that be because you live in Chicago?"

"No, I mean . . ."

"Roger, the committee has been meeting at the resort for twelve years now. Why change things when they're just getting going?" I said facetiously.

"Look, we may be snowed in." I said. But we can make use of the time. We've got the tourney all planned but we haven't reviewed the charitable list yet. Let's go over it and decide who gets what since we have to be here anyway."

"Well, I've got better things to do," Bridgett said. Bridgett was beautiful in a movie star fashion. Her thick blond hair, kept blond by expensive hairdressers, flowed across her soft shoulders and framed a near perfectly sculptured face, done at great expense by plastic surgeons from around the world. "I've got appointments and I have *got* to get out of here. Roger, honey, do something!"

"Do what, Bridgett? We're snowed in; can't you understand that? What the hell am I supposed to do?"

Bridgett screwed up her forehead until her thin eyebrows almost touched over the bridge of her tiny nose. She looked like she might be in pain but then an idea came to her and she brightened up. "Get one of those helicopters to come get us! How about it, honey?"

Roger spoke slowly so that his new wife would understand. "Bridgett," he said, "nothing is going to fly in this weather. Just accept the fact we're stuck here, OK?"

Bridgett was upset; I could tell by the pouting, down-turned lips and the fake sniffling meant to imitate crying. I was convinced she had forgotten how to really cry. The closest she could come was her baby-faced faked tears. Nobody rushed to her side to comfort her; it had taken only two days for everyone to get to know her for what she is.

The RV couple who were stranded with us were sitting nearby, but separated from the rest of us. Sandy went to them and introduced herself, inviting them to join us nearer the big fire.

The man was called Bobby Jim. His wife, equally blessed with a double name, that being Linda Sue, was . . . how do you say it? . . housewifely is probably the word. Bobby Jim had spent too much time making profits for the beer companies, proof of which was his too big belly that hung over his belted blue jeans that somehow complemented his thick and almost unkempt gray-black hair. But they were a friendly enough couple and spent an hour regaling us with their exploits behind the wheel of their big RV, having been seemingly almost everywhere in the U.S. that allows RVs.

Roger and Bridgett were the first to walk out, right in the middle of an exciting tale of the very best Texas chili in a dusty little town off some unknown and forgotten highway. Terry Adams followed them a few minutes later, tiptoeing out amidst a discussion of where the cheapest gasoline could be found.

Lyle Porter had found a bottle of brandy in a sideboard and was on his fourth snifter, ignoring the tales of the travelers. Marlene Adams and Sandy sat next to each other, both too nice to be impolite enough to leave. I slowly drifted toward Lyle, the idea of a little brandy in the coffee sounding really good right then.

As so often happens, good things are interrupted. Mrs. Albright, who ran the resort, entered the room and announced that lunch had been prepared.

The two travelers drifted off to their own table and the planning committee settled in at a bigger table on the far side of the room. Terry Adams returned but Roger and Bridgett didn't show up. In my opinion, lunch was better without them.

****

Sandy spent the afternoon washing and setting her beautiful brunette hair, which left me free to roam around the lobby lounge and play bartender to the two travelers, who preferred beer but were willing to try something harder. A few of the committee members began to show up. About three in the afternoon Roger and Bridgett came downstairs. They were not happy, to say the least. He was pushing chairs and tables around, she was scowling, and she had her arms folded tightly across her not in the least small breasts.

They settled for a small table away from everybody. Roger pulled a chair out for himself and slumped into it. Bridgett, accustomed to being treated better, stood by waiting for him to help her into a chair. He didn't, so she sat herself and turned her back to him.

"Thanks a lot, Roger," she snapped.

"Screw off," he answered.

"Don't talk to me like that, damn it."

"I'll talk to you any way I want," he growled. "So just screw off."

They were whispering through clenched teeth, but their voices carried across the big and almost empty room. With the arrival of Roger and his new wife, only Lyle Porter and Sandy were missing.

The resort had a short staff on duty: only Mrs. Albright, Annie who assisted Mrs. Albright in the kitchen, and Jennie Blake, who doubled as maid for the few rooms in use and helped out in the kitchen as needed. So I went from person to person, playing cocktail waiter, and mixing up what each person wanted.

When I got to Roger and Bridgett's table they were sitting with their backs to each other, deep in newly married argument.

"How about it," I said cheerfully. "Roger, I know you like a good dry vodka martini. How about you Bridgett?"

She brightened immediately and sat up in her chair. Her eyes veritably sparkled as she dove into the deepest of thought. I could almost hear the wheels grinding and the valves pushing and pulling as she weighed all the varied possibilities. Then she said, almost like a kid asking Santa for a Christmas wish, "I think I'll have a grasshopper! Can you do a grasshopper, Mr. Crew?"

"Please, call me Morgan," I said. "And I can do a grasshopper if you can drink a grasshopper. Have you had one before?"

"No, not really," she answered very seriously. "But it's green, isn't it? Green is like my favorite color right now. I used to like blue . . . but green seems to be popular right now."

"Yeah," I said. "I'll be right back."

Knowing Sandy liked vodka martinis, I mixed up a big crystal pitcher the way she liked them. There was enough for Sandy's one or two when she came downstairs, and the four or five I knew Roger would throw down before dinner.

Bobby Jim and his plump wife were easy; I just kept pitchers of beer coming for them. In between serving everyone I sipped on a good strong Wild Turkey 101 with just a splash of club soda while waiting for Sandy, whose appearance would brighten the room.

The afternoon dragged on and we all got just a little bit drunk, until about half past five when Sandy walked into the lounge. At her side was Mrs. Albright who looked worried about something. Sandy joined me at the bar and Mrs. Albright stood where everyone could see her.

"I have some bad news, I'm afraid," she said in a quavering voice. "I was on the phone to the sheriff. I was telling him we were stranded here. He confirmed that the roads out of the valley are all closed."

Everyone was silent; everyone was staring at Mrs. Albright, waiting for the other shoe that everyone sensed was about to drop. Rather than waiting amidst the pregnant silence, I said, "We kind of figured that out for ourselves, Mrs. Albright."

"There's more," she said. "The phone line went dead. We don't have any phones."

"No phones!" Terry Adams barked. "What the hell!"

"Terry, it's ok. The Sheriff knows we're here. Isn't that right Mrs. Albright?" I asked.

"Yes. And I'm sure he's getting together some trucks and plows to get to us. Please don't worry."

"No worry," Roger slurred, the three martinis plus the one he had in hand were working on him. "I got my cell phone." He pulled the small phone from the case fastened to his belt and held it up proudly for all to see. "Anybody needs to phone for pizza, you can use my phone . . . no charge."

I didn't have to let the light of truth shine on Roger's alcohol induced kindness, but I really like Roger very much, never had. So I took the opportunity to make him look dumb. "Sorry Rog," I said. "But there aren't any cell towers around here. Your phone isn't going to work."

Bridgett jumped up and did a poor job at a theatrical scream and said, "No cell phones! Oh no! What do we do?"

"Sit the hell down, Bridgett," Roger said disgustedly. "Don't make an ass out of yourself."

Bridgett sat, once again turning her back to her new husband. It seems each of Roger's marriages was shorter than the previous. I thought, as I leaned against the bar and sipped at my Wild Turkey, that this latest marriage might not outlast the snowstorm.

Terry was grumbling under his breadth about something, and Marlene was patting his arm and trying to calm him. Terry had always been one of the good people. He and I are regulars on the golf course. He hadn't had that much to drink to explain his mood, and I had never seen him so worried or nervous before. I shrugged it off by assuming everyone was a little worried about being snowed in thirty-five miles from the nearest civilization.

A thought suddenly occurred to me but I didn't want to toss more worry into the mix, so I waved Mrs. Albright over to the bar and asked her quietly, "With the phones down, are we going to lose electricity, too?"

"Oh, Mr. Crew," she whispered back to me. "It's already out."

I looked up at the lights shining brightly and questioned her with a look.

"I switched the generator on. It can run the whole place for seventy-two hours, more if we ration how we use power. But I don't want to worry anyone. I'm sure the roads will be cleared before then."

"Don't tell anyone," I agreed. "But switch off everything we don't need, just in case."

As an afterthought I asked, "How about fire wood?"

"We have plenty," she answered in a whisper.

"Let's keep fires going in the bedrooms and down here in the dining room and in the lounge," I said.

Mrs. Albright nodded and left the lounge, stopping at the door to turn and announce as an afterthought, "Oh yes. I almost forgot. We'll have dinner at half past six. It will be a very simple affair I'm afraid."

As she walked into the hallway Terry slammed his fist onto the tabletop sending a thunderclap reverberating through the lounge. Marlene flinched and bit her finger to stifle a scream. Terry kicked his chair over and stormed from the room.

Sandy ran to Marlene and took her in her arms. She was sobbing and had a hard time staying on her feet. Sandy helped her into a chair and sat beside her. I ran a glass of brandy to her; she took it gratefully and drank it down in one quick swallow.

Sitting at the table with the two women I took Marlene's hand and asked, "What's wrong? What's bothering Terry?"

"I don't know. I wish I did," she answered through her tears.

"I'll have a talk with him after dinner," I said. It seemed to please Marlene; she tried to smile as she dabbed at her eyes with a small, lacey hanky. When she had calmed a bit I made one last round, filling glasses and fetching another pitcher of beer for Bobby Jim, who was feeling pretty good by that time, laughing and singing some Country and Western tune I had never heard before. If it ain't jazz, I'm not interested!

At half past six I called to everyone to move into the dining room. Except for Sandy and me, everyone had a hard time walking straight, but everyone made it finally.

Jennie Blake had set one long table at which we all sat, the travelers at one end, the committee at the other, lest the peasants mix with the uppity-ups. Everyone was there . . . except for Lyle Porter, who hadn't showed up for drinks before dinner either. No one had seen him since after lunch.

Lyle wasn't the most sociable person around, but it was unlike him to miss dinner. I asked Annie to go to his room and tell him dinner was being served. We sat and Jennie Blake, a tall, very thin African-American woman of fifty years who could pass for thirty, served plates of simple green salad dressed nicely with a raspberry vinaigrette, followed by dishes of delicious chicken in a creamy mushroom sauce and lightly sautéed vegetables. It was a simple affair as Mrs. Albright promised, but delectable all the same.

We had just begun savoring the chicken when Annie ran into the room. She stumbled across the carpet, fell against a table and tipped over a chair. Her face was ashen, her mouth opened in a silent scream. Marlene and Sandy ran to her and held her arms before she could collapse to the floor. Everyone, I noticed, except Terry Adams, was on their feet.

"What is it?" Sandy asked Annie as she held onto her. "What's wrong?"

"Mr. Porter," she stammered in a fearsome whisper. "He's . . . he's . . . dead."

****

Sandy motioned to me to follow as she took Annie out of the dining room. Marlene returned to her husband, who was still seated, still holding his knife and chicken filled fork.

In the lobby we sat Annie in a chair. She looked up at us, a look of utter confusion and abject fear frozen across her face. Then the floodgates opened and a scream mixed with an ocean of tears burst forth.

It took a few minutes to calm her but we finally were able to get her to stand and take us to Lyle.

As we walked to the staircase leading up to the guest rooms, Sandy was able to get Annie to talk. She told us, "I went to Mr. Porter's room but he wasn't there. The room is a mess, things broken everywhere. I didn't know what to do. I went to the hallway but I didn't know where to look for Mr. Porter. I went back to his room and saw a light on in the bathroom, it was coming under the door, you know?"

We had reached Lyle's room and the three of us walked inside. The room was a mess as Annie had said. A fight must have taken place, although I couldn't picture Lyle as a fighter. The bathroom door was open and Annie pointed, telling us to go inside.

Sandy started for the bathroom. I'm more cautious than Sandy, some would say a coward, but my 'caution' has kept me alive all these years. I make it a habit *not* to rush in where angels fear to tread. I mean, if angels are smart enough not to rush into what might be danger, why should I?

So my hand on Sandy's arm stopped her and I slowly stepped towards the bathroom and gingerly peered around the door into the room. On the far side of the room was a big marble tub, just like the one in the room Sandy and I had. Except this big marble tub sported a pair of legs hanging over the edge.

Lyle Porter was in the tub, lying under water, his eyes wide and his mouth open in a death scream. A faint tinge of pink formed a lacey pattern in the water from a cut on the side of his head.

Sandy was beside me and took my arm. "Oh my God," she whispered. "Lyle. Why Lyle?"

"I don't know, Sandy. But we've got a lot of questions to ask."

A familiar voice sounded behind us. "What the hell's going on here?" It was Bobby Jim of the RV. He pushed Sandy and me aside and took two quick steps to the edge of the tub. After looking down at the submerged body for a second or two, he turned and said, "OK. This room is now sealed. Get the hell out."

The question I asked was obvious, "Who the hell *are* you?"

Bobby Jim pulled a battered leather case from his back pants pocket and flashed a silver badge and ID card at me. Before he could put it back in his pocket I quickly grabbed it from him and took a closer look at it.

"You're a retired cop," I said. "From someplace called Brighton, Oklahoma. Where the hell is Brighton, Oklahoma?"

"That ain't important," Bobby Jim answered and took his badge back. "Thing is, I'm the closest thing we got to a cop right now. And 'till the sheriff's guys get here, I'm in charge, get me?"

"Oh sure," Sandy said with a lot of sarcasm that was completely lost on Bobby Jim. "All we need now is a retired traffic cop from Bohunk County to find out who murdered Lyle."

"Ain't Bohunk County, lady. I ain't never heard of Bohunk County. Brighton's the County Seat. Might not be no New York or no California, but we got our share of killings. Now everybody out and back to the dining room. Nobody gets in here 'till the Sheriff gets here, understand?"

THE LINE

There wasn't much sense in arguing with Bobby Jim at that time. He had taken both Sandy and me by our arms and had ushered us out of the bathroom. He closed the bathroom door and pushed us into the hallway.

As he shepherded us towards the stairs I finally stopped him and said, "Bobby Jim, you can't leave the body in the water."

"Why not? The cops gotta see the evidence. Nothin' gets moved 'till the detectives see it and pictures are took. That's the way we done it in Brighton and that's the way we do it here, got it?"

Sandy tried to explain. "Look, we're snowed in here. It may be days before anyone gets to us. The body will deteriorate quickly in that water. Vital evidence may be lost."

"Bobby Jim," I said, "there are disposable cameras down in the lobby gift shop. I suggest we use them to photograph everything and then move the body out of the water. We can wrap it in sheets and keep it in the refrigerator."

"Why the refrigerator?" he asked.

"Because it will keep the body intact until the police arrive," Sandy explained. "The only thing we won't be able to determine is the time of death; they use body heat for that and the body heat will be lost after a few hours in the fridge. But all the other evidence will be preserved. We have to do it."

"Well . . . OK, I guess," Bobby Jim said. "Maybe you're right, I don't know. Let's get some cameras first. I know that's gotta' be done."

So we took three cameras from a rack in the little gift shop in the resort lobby and went back to Lyle's room. Bobby Jim used his to take 24 snaps of the body in the tub. He took every possible angle and then took each again. While he amused himself, Sandy and I looked through the wreckage of the room.

It appeared there had been a short brawl inside; a lamp and table had been knocked over, and we found spots of blood on the carpet near the bed. But the rest of the room had been tossed, searched by someone in a hurry who didn't care if anyone knew it had been searched.

Sandy took a few pictures of the blood spots, before they dried to a barely recognizable brown, and the broken lamp and table. We agreed there was no sense in worrying about preserving evidence in the bathroom. Bobby Jim was walking all over the place, destroying what might have been on the tile floor. He had washed his hands in the sink, used a towel to dry them, pissed in the toilet, flushed it and then washed his hands again. What the heck, that's probably how they do things in Brighton, Oklahoma.

When he was done, Bobby Jim joined us in the bedroom and sat on the bed before I could tell him not to. This guy seemed to have some penchant for destroying a crime scene.

"Look," he said, crossing his legs. "I still don't think we should be moving the body. It's important not to disturb stuff like that. I know. I spent thirty-six years wearing a badge."

I knew there wasn't any sense in getting Bobby Jim angry. Arguing with someone like that would only get his hackles up. But I had to get some sense into his thick skull. So I tried, as nicely as I could, to explain to him, "Bobby Jim, you walked all over the floor in the bathroom, you used the toilet, you washed your hands twice and used the towel. Nothing personal here, you know what you're doing, but do you think maybe the crime scene in the bathroom has been messed up just a little? Maybe I'm wrong, I mean, you're the expert."

Sandy wasn't quite as nice as I was. She was angry and as usual, she was ready to fight. "Look, damn it! If that body stays in the water for three or four days, there won't be anything left for the medical examiner to examine! Now get your fat ass off the bed and help us get Lyle somewhere safe!"

Bobby Jim looked shocked and he didn't know what to say. But he did get off the bed and started to pull the sheets from it.

"Not those sheets!" Sandy yelled. "From another room!"

It was a dirty and wet job, but between Bobby Jim and myself, we managed to get Lyle's body downstairs, using the service elevator, and into a big, walk-in refrigerator room off the kitchen. There was a long metal table inside. We placed him on it and made sure he was completely wrapped in several sheets we had taken from an unused guest room. I didn't want any part of Lyle's body touching the metal table directly. It wasn't the best thing that could be done with the body of a murder victim, but it was the only option we had.

There was no way to lock the door to the cold room so I just shrugged my shoulders in silent agreement with Sandy that there was nothing to be done about protecting the body.

We returned to the dining room to find it empty, the dinner plates remaining on the table filled with uneaten food. Jennie Blake was slowly clearing the table. She told us that Mrs. Albright had gathered everyone in the cocktail lounge to wait for the three of us to return. I cautioned Bobby Jim not to discuss anything about the murder or what we had found with anyone. I knew I didn't have to tell my wife that, she is

smart and we've been hip deep in murders before. But I
wasn't sure about Bobby Jim. He answered, "Sure, damn, I
know that. I'm a cop, remember?"

When we walked into the lounge Bobby Jim
announced loudly, "Jesus H. Christ! What a mess! The guy
was drowned!" So much for not announcing anything.

****

Sandy and I retreated to a far corner of the cocktail
lounge, to a small table near a window overlooking the snow
covered patio and swimming pool.   In short course we
decided that a drink and something to munch on was called
for, so while I mixed a vodka martini and a Wild Turkey and
club soda, Sandy hunted down a jar of peanuts from behind
the bar.

At the table we talked about what needed to be done.

"Nobody is going anywhere," I argued. "Let's just wait
for the sheriff to get here and let him figure out what
happened."

"Morgan," Sandy said, as usual exasperated at my
attempts of keeping my nose out of other people's problems.
"Face it. We have probably a small town, country sheriff
who had a career directing plows over thirty-five miles of
two-lane road. He probably did that job very well, but solving
a murder? It's up to us, Morgan."

"Why? I mean, Lyle wasn't that close to us. He really
wasn't a friend."

"Doesn't make any difference," she said. "He was
murdered and the murderer is right here with us. If the roads
get opened, whoever killed him might get away. We have
the opportunity to find out who did it and turn him . . . or her .
. . over to the police when they get here."

I could have gone on for hours. I could have raised

one point after another, arguing rationally why we should keep our noses out of other people's problems. But two undefeatable obstacles were always in my way when I tried to stay out of trouble: the fact that I am a sucker for helping people when they need help, and the fact that my wonderful wife has become bent on solving every problem she and I run into. So, rather than waste the evening I just gave in, as usual.

"OK," I said. "Where do we start?"

"Before I met you I would not have known where to start. But living with you has taught me some stuff. Motive, means and opportunity, dear. Let's start filtering out people until we know who killed Lyle."

"There's one more thing I wish you could learn, Sandy. Let's not get ourselves killed."

"Oh, Morgan! We aren't going to get killed," she said and laughed off my warning.

"Sandy, you ran for your life in San Marcos. Remember what happened in Las Vegas? And those bloodthirsty killers in London? We've been chased by death since we've known each other."

"Yeah," she said, smiling slyly and very sexy. "And ain't it fun?"

So we were off again, despite my better judgment and despite that little voice in the back of my head yelling at me to run away. I figured we had about two days, three at the outside. The snow had to stop sooner or later, and the Sheriff would have plows working. Maybe, just maybe, I could keep Sandy stumbling around long enough for the plows to get there and for the Sheriff to take over. And maybe, just maybe, we would both be alive when that happened.

Sandy sipped gently at the vodka martini, and I threw down the bourbon in one quick swallow. "Here's what we have to do," Sandy said as I coughed on the drink. "We have to figure out who had opportunity first. There's not much use trying to do background on these folks while we're stuck here. So let's use a process of elimination. Lyle was at lunch, but we didn't see him since then. Where was everybody from lunch time on?"

"I don't know," I answered. "I wasn't paying much attention."

Without hesitation Sandy turned and walked across the room to the waiting guests.

"OK," she announced in a commanding voice. "We need to know where everyone was from when we had lunch to now."

We spent over an hour questioning everyone. It wouldn't have taken so long had it not been for good ol' Bobby Jim. He interrupted countless times, and every few minutes he "explained" why we were asking certain questions. The whole thing would have taken maybe ten minutes without his help.

But it was soon apparent that we weren't getting anywhere. Everyone had an alibi and nobody was alone for more than a few minutes. Unless Lyle hit himself over the head and then drowned himself after fighting with himself and destroying the room, somebody had to have killed him. If we were to believe all the alibis, the killer wasn't in the lounge that night.

"And if the killer isn't here," Sandy whispered, reading my mind, "then it has to be either Mrs. Albright, Jennie or Annie."

As I took a swallow of bourbon I nodded slightly. I couldn't believe it, but it had to be. If the ten guests all had alibis, and if Sandy and I didn't kill Lyle, and since we were snowed in so no one could get into the resort, that left only the three employees. But I had to get an answer to a question that had been burning through my mind for a long time. I left Sandy and walked to Terry Adams, asking him to join me at the bar were we could talk in private.

"Terry," I said. "You've been in a rotten mood the last

couple of days. You and Marlene are in the middle of some kind of argument. That's not natural . . . for you, I mean. You and Marlene have been happy together as long as I've known you. What's up?"

"None of your business, Morgan. Leave me alone," he snapped.

He started to walk away but I grabbed his arm and held him back.

"It may be my business," I said. "I need to find out who killed Lyle and I don't believe in coincidences. You and Marlene being at odds and Lyle's death may or may not be connected. Convince me they aren't connected."

"You always have to stick that nose of yours into everybody's business, don't you? OK, Morgan. I'll tell you. Marlene is sick. She has cancer and she's dying. I'm pissed off because she refuses to do anything about it."

"My God! I'm so sorry. But what won't she do?"

"The doctors say it's not operable. I want her to go to Europe, to a clinic that uses experimental treatments. They have been having great results. But she won't." Tears began to cloud his eyes and his voice broke. He leaned against the bar to keep his knees from buckling and whispered, "I don't want to lose her, Morgan."

I'm not good around sick people and grieving people. I never know what to say or do, and I'm always afraid I will say the wrong things. So I said nothing but I did put my arms around him and held him as he fought back the tears.

Terry pushed himself away from me quickly, regained full composure, and returned to his wife. I went back to Sandy and in a whispered voice, told her why Terry was angry.

So we tried to ease our way out of the lounge, but in the hallway the heavy footsteps of Bobby Jim followed us.

"Yeah," he said loudly. "I got the same idea you got. Got to be one of the dames works here, right?"

"Look, Bobby Jim," I tried. "How about leaving this to

us. The ladies work for me, after all."

"This here is police work. You two better go back to the lounge and wait there," he said as he pushed his way past us. But Sandy is not to be deterred, by anything or anybody. She grabbed Bobby Jim's arm at his big bicep with both her hands and shoved him against the wall of the hallway. She then led a very quiet and demur Bobby Jim and me to the kitchen.

There we found Mrs. Albright supervising and helping Annie and Jennie wash dishes and scrub pans. The three women were subdued and occasionally wiped away a tear as they worked. They each turned to see the three of us walk through the swinging butler's doors and into the big black and white checkerboard floored room.

Before Bobby Jim could open his trap, Sandy stepped forward and said, "I am very sorry to bother you ladies, but we need to ask a few questions."

"Why, what kind of questions?" Mrs. Albright asked authoritatively. She was immediately taking a protective stance between her employees and us. That would present a problem, but I would have been surprised if she hadn't done this.

"We have asked all the guests," Sandy said, "and now we need to know where each of you were from when we had lunch to when dinner was served."

"Are you accusing one of us? . . ."

"I'm not accusing anyone of anything," Sandy said. She smiled gently and took a step toward Mrs. Albright, but the resort manager pulled away and stepped backward, wringing a dishtowel in her hands. "We just need to know."

"Because someone killed Mr. Porter," Annie said, her voice weak and quavering. "And it has to be someone here at the lodge."

"That's right Annie," I said. She didn't look frightened at the realization; she had stated a fact that she had kept silently inside of her up to then.

"Well," she said, setting a half washed sauté pan down on a broad wooden prep table, letting the soap and water run from the pan onto the maple. "It wasn't one of us. We were all working together all afternoon."

That's right," Mrs. Albright said stepping to Annie's side and placing her arm around the girl's shoulders. "We've been working very hard to keep your guests happy, Mr. Crew. There's just the three of us, you know. We'll be putting in twelve and fourteen-hour days keeping you happy until we get out of here. I find it offensive that you could accuse us."

"You're not being accused of anything, Mrs. Albright," Sandy said. "We just need to find out where everyone was."

"That's a job for the police," Mrs. Albright said strongly. "You have no right to ask such questions."

"Well, I'm the police," Bobby Jim said loudly. "I might be retired but I still have some authority . . . At least until the Sheriff gets here." He looked from one woman to the next, scowling like he thought a tough street cop might scowl. I had no doubt that he was just acting. "So start answering the questions," he demanded. "Account for your whereabouts. You first, Albright."

"That's Mrs. Albright," I said. "Show some respect."

"Yeah, whatever," he said, brushing aside my demand.

Mrs. Albright tossed her towel on the counter next to the sink, straightened up proudly, and said, "Let's see. While you people were enjoying the lunch we prepared for you, the three of us were here, in the kitchen. Jennie had opened a couple of cans of soup. Annie put together a few cheese sandwiches. We ate quickly because we had to make sure you people were happy. We didn't have time to waste. After that we cleared your table and washed the dishes."

"And after that?" Bobby Jim asked.

Annie spoke up, still seemingly unafraid, "After that I

helped Jennie finish making up your rooms. She didn't have enough time to finish them before we had to start thinking about dinner."

"How about you?" Bobby Jim asked gruffly, looking at Mrs. Albright.

"I went to the cupboard to see what we had for dinner."

"So you were alone?" Bobby Jim growled. "How do we know you didn't use that time to kill Lyle Porter?"

Sandy and I both turned on Bobby Jim at the same time. "Wait a damn minute!" I shouted. "Lyle was forcibly drowned! Someone beat the crap out of him then held him under water to drown him. Look at Mrs. Albright. Does she look capable of beating up and drowning a man half her age?"

Bobby Jim actually had to take time to think about that one. After a moment or two he conceded, "OK, so that's not likely. But I ain't gonna forget. The Sheriff might be interested."

Then he turned to Annie and asked, "So you and her were together . . . for how long? How long did it take to finish the rooms?"

"More than an hour. Some of you guests returned to your rooms after your lunch and messed things up, then told us to straighten up again." Annie stopped suddenly and her face went ashen for a split second. I caught it, Sandy caught it, and unfortunately Bobby Jim caught it, too.

An uncomfortable and almost deadly silence fell across the kitchen. Annie was no poker player; she couldn't hide the realization that had come to her. She knew something important, something that would throw suspicion on someone.

Bobby Jim took two long and quick steps to Annie, grabbed her arms in his big hands and held on tightly. "OK," he sneered, "Tell me what you know."

Annie shook herself free of his grip and backed away.

She was scared now, frightened of what she had thought of. Sandy pushed Bobby Jim aside, glared at him angrily, and went to Annie. She held Annie's hands in hers and said softly, "If you know something, you have to tell us, Annie."

Before Annie could speak, Jennie stepped forward. Her face was streaked with tears; she was biting the soft, fleshy base of her thumb.

"Annie just remembered that I wasn't with her all that time. You remember," she said, nodding toward Bobby Jim. "You asked that I light a fire in your room. I went and got my coat and boots and went outside to get an armload of wood. I had to cut some kindling; there wasn't none out there. I was gone about twenty minutes or so. But I didn't kill nobody," she said, starting to sob. "You gotta believe me, Mr. Crew. I didn't kill nobody."

"I believe you, Jennie," I said. She rushed into my arms and I held her softly as she cried. Jennie was a thin woman, although she was tall. As I held her I could feel little muscle in her. I could not believe that she could have overpowered even Lyle Porter. But it was the first time we had found anyone without an alibi for their time.

Bobby Jim realized that, too. And he jumped on the fact.

"You ever been arrested, girl?" he asked with a nasty grin on his face.

I kept my arm around Jennie's shoulders and said to Bobby Jim, "Watch it old man. Jennie is not a girl; she's a woman, a lady. And I believe her."

"Yeah, well I don't. And I think I better keep an eye on her until the Sheriff gets here."

"Where's she going to go?" I demanded. "We're snowed in here, remember?"

"Yeah, well I'm gonna keep my eye on her anyway. She's the only one who got no alibi."

THE SINKER

That night was tense and few words were spoken by anyone. A light meal, in lieu of the uneaten dinner, was served. A platter of cold meats and cheeses, and a little green salad. I had hoped for something better but after what had occurred in the kitchen, I was thankful for what we got.

I found several of bottles of passable Napa Valley Cabernet and made sure everyone's glass was kept full. But nobody noticed and nobody cared. Bobby Jim gulped down the wine with mouthfuls of food, not wanting to waste the time necessary to actually taste anything.

Jennie was nowhere to be seen. Mrs. Albright and Annie rushed about, Annie in tears, Mrs. Albright angry. Bobby Jim and his wife felt the discomfort of the rest of us but gave no thought of honoring our silence. He stuffed his face with everything that was brought to the table and looked around for more. He bragged to anyone who would halfway listen of having "solved another one". The two of them laughed and made snide, racist remarks that were insulting to the resort's hard working staff and us.

My guests drifted off alone or in pairs, all winding up in the lounge, standing around the bar, hoping Bobby Jim and Linda Sue wouldn't join us. And I admit it; I wanted to get drunk. But one glance from Sandy changed my mind. She knew something that she wanted me to know, and since I trust her absolutely, I knew I had to keep a clear head for at least a while longer. Unfortunately, Bobby Jim and his wife slammed into the lounge demanding booze.

When everyone was comfortably ensconced in their third or fourth drinks, Sandy gently pulled me off to the side of the room, where we could talk without being overheard. She whispered, "I was talking with Mrs. Alright. She's very upset."

"I can understand that," I answered. "Everybody except Bobby Jim seems to be upset. We're trapped here . . . with a killer."

"That's not what I mean. She told me about Jennie Blake."

"What about her?"

Sandy looked over my shoulder to make sure no one was nearby or near enough to hear. "Jennie Blake is on parole."

"Parole!" I said too loudly. Sandy hushed me and went on, "Mrs. Albright said she was in prison for three years . . . on a manslaughter charge. Mrs. Albright knew Jennie's mother. She gave Jennie a job here when no one else would hire her."

"Manslaughter," I said. "That doesn't sound good. Kind of works into Bobby Jim's accusations."

"Mrs. Albright doesn't believe it and neither do I. I think we need to sneak off and talk to Jennie alone."

"Was she guilty?" I asked.

"Mrs. Albright said Jennie had been drinking and got into an auto accident. Someone died. Jennie made no excuses to Mrs. Albright."

We stayed in the corner for another half hour, waiting and watching. We didn't want Bobby Jim tagging along when we spoke with Jennie.

The people in the lounge were quiet for the most part, except of course for Bobby Jim. He was happy and drunk, and he was grabbing at his plump little wife who seemed to be enjoying it. At least she was giggling and wiggling, and not exactly pushing him away. After tossing down two more drinks, Bobby Jim dragged her from the lounge, without complaints from her, and loudly announced that he was taking her back to their room to "do her real good". Very romantic stuff.

A few minutes later the others started filtering out and going to their rooms. When Sandy and I were alone in the lounge, we turned off the lights and made our way to Jennie Blake's room. I wasn't as sure of her innocence as Sandy seemed to be. But I was willing to accept the fact that Sandy was seldom wrong about anything. If she felt Jennie was innocent, then maybe she was.

Sandy knocked gently on Jennie's door. There was no answer so she knocked again, then a third time. I tried the knob and found the door unlocked. Pushing the door open, we were greeted by darkness and silence and a rush of very cold air.

"Jennie," Sandy called out. "Jennie, it's Sandy Crew. Can I speak with you?"

There was no answer. "She isn't here," I said. "Let's go to the kitchen. She's probably there."

"It's too cold in there, Morgan," Sandy said. "There's something wrong."

Sandy quickly pushed the door open and stepped inside with me closely behind. It was freezing cold inside and dark, the only light being moonlight coming through the open window across the room.

Jennie was not in the room. I went to the open window to close it. As I stretched to pull the sash down something caught my eye. There was a shadow in the moonlit snow three floors below. I looked down and saw the misshapen body of Jennie Blake lying in a hole in the white snow.

****

We quietly ran down the stairs and out the rear door, onto the ice and snow covered back deck. Jennie's room was to our left and a long way away, near the far corner of the building. We trudged through the snow that had drifted against the building several feet deep. We had not stopped to put on boots or coats or anything to protect us from the weather and cold night air.

It was hard work getting through the knee-deep snow, and within a moment or two we were soaked through to our skin. A light snow was falling but there was no wind. The air was very cold and we were shivering.

It took a long time but we finally made it to Jennie. I didn't have to feel for a pulse; she was lying face up, her arms and legs were twisted in unnatural directions, her eyes were open wide and her mouth was frozen in a silent scream. There was a small blotch of red blood in the snow beneath Jennie's left ear.

Sandy, too, knew that Jennie was dead. She stood a few feet behind me, her hand covering her mouth in shock. "What are we going to do, Morgan?" she whispered. "We can't leave her here."

"I don't want Bobby Jim's help. Go back inside and get Terry and Roger. We'll take her inside and put her with Lyle. And get more sheets . . . and another disposable camera," I said as an afterthought. "I'll wait here."

"I'll bring back some coats and boots," Sandy said as she turned and did the best she could to run through the snow.

We took twenty-four photos of Jennie's body from every conceivable angle, and we three men managed to carry her into the house and place her carefully next to Lyle's colorless corpse. I decided to make some surreptitious checking on everyone at the resort.

I went from room to room, easing open each door, and found that except for myself and Sandy, and Terry and Roger, everyone was snoring away peacefully. I made Terry and Roger promise to go back to bed and not speak with anyone. Breakfast would be the time to gather everyone together and to try to delve out who was killing people in our snowbound trap.

As breakfast was being laid out in the big dining room, I asked Sandy to go with Annie, Mrs. Albright's only remaining employee and go from room to room and wake everyone. Soon all the guests were seated and I asked Mrs. Albright and Annie to join us at the table.

"OK," I said. "We're all here."

"No we ain't," Bobby Jim injected. "The black girl, where's she at?"

"That's why we're here," I answered and glanced at Sandy. "Jennie Blake is dead."

Mrs. Albright screamed; Annie stood and tried to scream but found only a muted whimper and a flood of tears. A few forks dropped and several people mumbled 'No!' and other meaningless things. Bobby Jim laughed and shouted, "Killed herself, huh! Just what I figured she'd do! She knew I had her dead to rights!"

"Unless she beat herself over her head and then tossed herself out a window, I doubt she killed herself," I said.

Realization spread slowly through the room. People looked at each other, from one blank, cold face to another. There was a killer sitting at the table.

I let that fact set in amongst them and watched each person carefully. Everyone was scared, that was easy to see. But I needed to filter out the fear of sitting next to a murderer from the fear of a murderer being trapped. I glanced at Sandy and saw she was doing the same thing I was, peering deeply at each person's reaction. I hoped that between the two of us we could stop the killer before he . . or she . . . could kill again.

Bobby Jim broke the mood, as I anticipated he would do. "OK," he said as he stood slowly to his feet. "Seems to me we got us a murderer right here in this room. Ain't no way around it. So I'm going to interrogate every damn one of you. And I know all the tricks. If I gotta' beat the truth out of one of you, well that's just what I'm gonna' do."

"You're not going to hit anyone," I said, trying to sound authoritative and in charge. "It won't take much longer for the Sheriff to get here. Maybe even today. Until that time, we just all stay together. If nobody is alone, then nobody can be hurt. Does everyone agree?"

"Hell no!" Bobby Jim shouted. "I'm in charge here! We do as I tell ya'!"

"You're in charge of nothing, Bobby Jim. This is my resort; I own it. You're standing on my floor. You're eating my food. You're breathing my damn air. Now sit down and shut that big fat mouth of yours before . . ." I hesitated, not from being scared but because I don't like making threats. They are all too often too hard to back up.

"Before you do what?" he challenged.

"Before I let my wife beat the crap out of you."

That shut him up, I think because he didn't know how to respond to it. Sandy tried valiantly to hide her beaming grin behind her hand. And the others at the table all began to laugh, at first nervously, then, finding the laughter a good release of tension, threw themselves into sidesplitting guffaws.

We spent the day together, mostly in silence, everyone knowing that being bored was better than being dead.

Lunch was sandwiches prepared in the kitchen by Mrs. Albright and Annie, with Sandy and Marlene helping out while everyone else stood around watching. We played cards and checkers and chess and whatever other games were available after lunch. Before dinner we all needed a few drinks, so everyone nearly ran to the bar where Bobby Jim and his wife tossed down more beer then I thought was possible for two ordinary people to swallow. Before anyone could get too drunk I shuffled everyone off to the kitchen once again where cans of soup were opened and heated. No one had much of an appetite.

I then shepherded my flock back to the bar. My idea was to keep everyone together until all or most were pleasantly zonkered, then parade them to their rooms and see them to bed. I insisted that Mrs. Albright and Annie share a guest room rather than go to their own rooms downstairs, near the kitchen.

I would spend the night in a chair in the hallway outside the bedrooms to make sure everyone stayed put and nobody else met the grim reaper . . . whoever the grim reaper was.

Sandy insisted that I was not going to pull sentry duty alone. We pulled two chairs close together in the hallway near a small table. Sandy retrieved a plate of various cheeses from the kitchen and brought a huge pot of hot and very strong coffee with the plate to the hallway. I had already sneaked a full bottle of Wild Turkey 101 from the bar, and we found that a liberal splash of bourbon in a cup of coffee made the coffee very tasty indeed.

As we sat and wished the hours would pass faster, Sandy asked suddenly, "So, who killed Lyle?" She always came right to the point, no beating around the bush for her. And her pointed question also told me that she had her own ideas about who the killer was. I would play the game with her.

"Why just Lyle?" I asked. "Jennie Blake was killed, too, you know."

"I know," she answered sarcastically. "But her death was the result of Lyle's. She knew something or maybe saw something. Whoever killed Lyle, killed her. So if we find out who killed Lyle, we have her murderer, too."

"OK, so who killed Lyle?"

"Elimination my dear. If we eliminate whoever didn't or couldn't have done it, then we will be left with who did."

"You've been reading Sherlock Holmes, haven't you?" I asked.

"I read those stories years ago, when I was a girl. Even so, the theory is right, isn't it?"

"So go on," I said. "There's something spinning around in that beautiful head of yours."

"There are eight people who could have killed Lyle. Terry and Marlene Adams; Roger and Bridgett Townsend; Bobby Jim and . . . what's his wife's name? And of course, Mrs. Albright and Annie."

That's right," I agreed. "But you can't suspect Mrs. Albright. And Annie just doesn't seem to be the type. She's . . . she's . . ."

"Too gentle?" Sandy suggested. "I agree. I don't see her as the type. She's too emotional and I don't think anyone could act good enough to pass themselves off as soft and as scared as she is. And I don't for a minute think Mrs. Albright could have done it. How long has she been working for you?"

"Longer than I can remember. I think my father hired her."

"Besides, what motive would either have? Neither Roger nor Terry liked Lyle very much. And could Mrs. Albright or Annie . . . or even both working together over power Lyle? I don't think so."

"Not liking someone is not reason for murder," I injected.

"That's true. But I think I know something that might stretch not liking into hatred. You noticed that Roger and his new wife, Bridgett, aren't getting along very well? I know why," she said smugly. Sandy leaned back in her chair and grinned the grin of a very satisfied and knowledgeable person.

Since she was obviously waiting for me to ask her what she knew, and since I know her well enough to know that she would wait hours, even days if necessary, for me to ask, I decided not to waste time. "OK," I said. "Why?"

"Before Rog and Bridgett were married, she was involved with Lyle."

"By involved, you mean . . ."

"Every inch of involved, my dear. They had a hot and heavy relationship for a few months, before and after the date that she and Roger announced their wedding date. Roger found out and suspects the affair never ended."

"But I thought . . ."

"You thought Lyle was gay, right? Maybe he was but he liked Bridgett and she seemed to like him."

The evidence to prove the truth of what Sandy told me was unnecessary, at least at that time. I know Sandy very well, and I know that when she says something, she is sure of it. Gossip and rumors are anathema to her. If she didn't know for a fact that Lyle and Bridgett were sexually involved, she wouldn't have said so. I would leave the proof to the police. She would give them the details.

"You're not going to tell Bobby Jim are you?" I asked.

"Are you kidding?

THE CATCH

That night was interminably long. Sandy and I sat in the hallway as the others slept. It rapidly got cold, and Sandy retrieved a couple of wool blankets from our room. The blankets were great but I was intent on letting the bourbon keep me warm. As it turned out, I once again gave in to Sandy when she took the still half full bottle from me and placed it on the floor near her feet, where she could protect it from me.

Gray light began to filter in through frosted windows. I was fighting to stay awake and Sandy had taken to walking up and down the hallway, her blanket wrapped around her shoulders, to try to stay awake. But it turned out to be worth it as no one else died.

Morning brought a clear day, the first day without clouds and snow since we had arrived. The guests started to wake, and one by one they filtered downstairs to the dining room where Mrs. Albright and Annie had managed to lay out a breakfast of eggs, bacon, toast, and various fruits. I ignored the fact that the eggs were overdone and the bacon burnt and the coffee too weak. The two ladies had as much on their mind as everyone else did. Bobby Jim, of course, complained.

There was not much conversation around the big table as we finished the coffee. I was wondering what we would do that day, how I could keep everyone together, when I first heard the rumbling.

Within seconds everyone at the table heard it and Annie raced into the room yelling excitedly, "They're here! The snow plows are here!"

Outside, we all stood in the bitterly cold winter air, stomping our feet and hugging ourselves to try to stay warm. We joked gleefully and watched the two big trucks with huge plows in front, pushing eight or ten feet of snow to the side. Salvation had arrived and no one else would die. And behind the trucks were two green and white Sheriff's cars.

Inside, near the warmth thrown off by a big fire in the stone fireplace in the lounge, we sat, some feeling content and safe, others feeling like they should not be held there. The Sheriff of Cobalt County, Stan Weaver, assured everyone that they would be taken out of the valley that day. He told us that the weather forecast was for two days of clearing skies before another storm front moved in. But he wanted statements from everyone first.

The two bodies were placed in body bags and taken out to one of the cars. Sheriff Weaver had his statements from everyone except Sandy and me. He approached us uneasily and said, "Mr. Crew, I'm sorry, but I need to get a statement from the two of you, too. Do you mind?"

"Why would I mind?" I asked him, knowing the answer already.

"It's just . . . well, you know . . ."

"Sheriff, there's no need to show us any deference."

"But Mr. Crew . . ."

I chose to let it slide. All my life, because of the money my family name controls, people have thought it necessary to treat me like some kind of European royalty. I used to get upset and snap heads off when people did that to me. Now I just feel sorry for them.

"Sheriff, my wife has something to tell you. Someone here has a motive to kill Lyle Porter."

We walked with the Sheriff to the other side of the room and Sandy told him what she had told me.

"Are you sure about that?" he asked her when she had finished her story.

"Yes.   Several people told me . . . before Roger married Bridgett. I suppose it's common knowledge. I can give you some names if you'd like."

Sheriff Weaver went to Roger Townsend and told him he would have to return to town with him for further questioning.   He waived to one of his deputies who took Roger outside and to one of the Sheriff's cars.   Roger shouted and yelled and threatened, but he wasn't stupid enough to resist the steal-clamp grip of the deputy on his arm.   Bridgett complained loudly to no avail, although there were no tears from her. She seemed more inconvenienced than worried about her husband.

"Who the hell is going to drive me out of this damn place!" she demanded.

Eventually everyone left the resort, leaving Mrs. Albright and Annie to clean up and lock up before they, too, left later that day. All seemed to be at a conclusion . . . except for the fact that I didn't believe for a minute that Roger Townsend killed Lyle and Jennie.

Sandy and I drove out of the valley on the cleared road. We were silent as we watched the snow covered scenery glide by. As we reached the highway and settled into a cruise-controlled three-hour drive, Sandy turned to me and asked, "So, who the hell killed them?"

"I haven't the foggiest idea, my dear," I answered.

****

Bobby Jim whistled as he steered the big RV out of the valley and towards the highway. He drove slowly, being careful of the still ice-slick road, and let the others pass him one by one in their fancy luxury cars. He waved to each as they passed and sneered at their cars, such obvious shows of wealth. How stupid!

Linda Sue was relaxing in the big front passenger seat of the RV. She had put a CD of some country-western music in the player and cranked the volume up too loud.

She turned to Bobby Jim and said, "So when do I get my other five hundred bucks?"

"Soon as we get back to L.A. I told you that."

"Are you sure no one is going to know? I mean, what if the cops find out?"

"Townsend doesn't know who I am. He knows me as Bobby Jim.   He actually thinks I'm an ex-cop from Oklahoma. And he really thinks you're my wife. There's no way we can be traced."

"But he'll talk," the woman who had been called Linda Sue said.

"He'll talk, alright. He'll eventually confess that he hired a killer to murder Lyle Porter. He'll tell them all about the affair Porter was having with his wife. It won't make any difference. We can't be traced."

"But why the black girl?" she asked. "I still don't get that."

"Years ago . . . I knew her brother. I met her. It took me awhile to remember where I had seen her before. I don't think she remembered me or would recognize me, but I couldn't take any chances."

The woman shrugged her shoulders, not really caring. She had gotten fifteen hundred dollars already and another five hundred would be coming her way. All she had to do was to pretend to be this guy's wife. No sex, of course. She had made that clear from the beginning. It was easy money.

As the last vehicle from the resort, carrying Mrs. Albright and Annie, passed them Bobby, Jim waved and smiled and waited for it to move on out of sight. He slowed the RV and braked easily, still careful of the icy road. He pulled the RV to a stop at the side of the road and turned off the engine.

"Why are we stopping?" the woman asked. She turned to look at Bobby Jim but all she saw was the first flash of the gun as the professional killer currently known as Bobby Jim shot her in the head and chest four times.

He dragged her lifeless body from the RV and pushed her into a snow bank at the side of the road. It would be many months before a thaw would reveal her corpse. The only person who could be a witness against him was now dead.

Bobby Jim got back into the RV, having to pull himself up the steps. He opened his coat and shirt and pulled off the uncomfortable and restricting stage-prop vest with the protruding stuffed belly that had made him look so fat. He used the RV's sink to wash the gray out of his hair. Looking in the mirror above the sink, he once again recognized himself. The thirty-four year old killer, slim and muscular, was himself again.

Behind the wheel, he started the engine, tossed the country-western CD out the window into the snow, and drove away.

THE END

SPRING KILL

THE HOOK

The winter proved to be long and cold every place we went. We were trying to get away from that winter in Montana. We drove my old MGB south out of San Marcos to L. A. and then San Diego, but we couldn't escape the cold.

We tried Phoenix and we tried Santa Fe, but somehow, in spite of the heat, we found the lingering memory remained with us of the snow and cold, and the deaths that came with it in the Montana hills. I think Sandy just wanted to keep on the move. I think she hoped seeing something new every morning might keep the nightmares away.

Death and violence seemed to be following us like an albatross. We saw the skeletal form of The Grim Reaper, draped in his black shroud and carrying his scythe in every shadow

There was a dark cloud over our heads that only we could see. But it was there no matter where we went. We awoke in the morning and went to bed at night knowing that right behind us, just over our shoulders, was more trouble waiting to crash down on our heads.

It was one thing to help people who needed help. I accepted the fact that we – Morgan and Sandy Crew – were still the go-to people when someone needed something they couldn't do for themselves. And Sandy still wanted to help people. "Why be so rich if you can't use it for some good," she would argue.

As for me, I was sick and tired of being the fall guy. All I wanted to do was to say "NO!" when somebody – friend or family – came to me. If I wasn't so sure poverty was damn hard, I would give up all the money and go to work somewhere. Maybe then they'd leave me alone.

But that wasn't going to happen.

And so we drove on, outwardly hoping to find some warm weather but inwardly, unspoken by both Sandy and me, we were running away from that black clad monster called Death.

We were driving east along I-20 when we reached the outskirts of Dallas. It was then that Sandy had an idea.

"Hey," she said. "You know, I've never been down to the Keys. Let's go there."

So we found our way to the Rosewood Mansion at Turtle Creek outside of Dallas, checked into a suite and made some reservations.

I found a shipping company that would truck my MGB back to San Marcos. Sandy booked two first class tickets to Miami but made them for the following weekend which gave us two full days to rest and relax at the Rosewood.

****

At Miami International we rented a nice little Mercedes convertible and started down Highway 1. The traffic was light and I drove slowly as we enjoyed the cool breeze off the Gulf. It was past noon and hunger was finding its way to us. We had passed Islamorada and were approaching Gato Key, which is a small island along the chain.

Sandy suggested we turn off when she saw a ratty looking fish bar sitting on a spit of sand. It was just about the only building of any size on Gato Key. But that ratty looking fish bar served up some fine deep fried fish and bowls of steamed shrimp and huge pan seared scallops, all of which we stuffed ourselves with, along with several bottles of ice cold beer.

We moved from under the tattered palm thatched roof to a small aged wooden deck just a few feet over the Gulf's water. Sandy stretched out under the sun and said, "Now this is more like it, Morgan. I vote we stay here forever."

"I second that motion," I said and drained my third bottle of beer. "The only problem is there isn't any place to check into around here."

We were interrupted by the bartender who brought us two more bottles of the icy beer.

"There ain't no motels or nothin' nearby," he said as he placed the two bottles on a small table. "You're gonna hafta' drive quite a ways back north. That's the closest."

Oh, that's too bad, Sandy said. "It's so quiet and lovely here."

"You wanna' stay here? I don't get it but if you do I got this here 48' Warner."

Sandy looked at me questioningly. I said, "That's a motor yacht. Nice one, too . . . if it's not too old."

"Just bought it new last year. My old lady's uncle kicked off and left her some money, ya' know?"

"So you rent it out?" I asked.

"When I can," he said. "You guys like to fish?"

Sandy was about to laugh because she knows of my affliction for dropping a line in the water. But then memories of Cap'n Nick flooded back and a tear sparkled in her beautiful eye.

"How much?" I asked.

He thought for a moment, glancing at my Rolex and Sandy's expensive jewelry, and then said, "One night . . . a hunnert' bucks."

I suppose that was a great deal of money to him, but I decided to bargain and have some fun.

"Suppose we want it for a week?" I asked. How about five hundred for the week?"

"Five hunnert'!" he said. "Sure . . . five hunnert would be just fine."

****

The boat, named 'Good Luck', was in good shape, fairly clean and the fuel tanks were almost full. We stocked it with wine and bourbon and vodka, and promised ourselves that we would catch enough fish with the tackle onboard and dive for enough lobsters to keep us fed.

And off we went, doing our best to forget. I'm only fairly good at navigation but the boat had a good computer controlled satellite navigation system.

With Sandy's inevitable help I plugged in a course that would take us south, past Key West. We had some fun up on the flying bridge steering after switching off the auto pilot.

It was late in the afternoon so as Sandy handled the wheel I dropped two lines off the aft hoping to catch some dinner. I knew that we could always turn around and pull in to Key West and have a nice dinner, which is what we wound up doing. Plus, we stayed to listen to some pretty loud music and drink too many fruity and silly rum drinks.

Around two in the morning we staggered back onto

The Good Luck and fell onto the big bed in the forward cabin. By noon we were back underway, Key West at our backs.

The sea was calm, the sky clear and bright blue. The GPS was set to take us to The Bahamas where we would refill the fuel tanks and stock up on some food. But too many tall rum drinks the night before stayed with us into the late afternoon. So we pulled next to a small sandy atoll – of which there are hundreds in the Caribbean, most treeless, without water and uninhabited.

I dropped the forward and aft anchors keeping us a hundred feet from the shallow, sandy bottom. I was finishing a bottle of beer when Sandy said, "OK, boss man, what do we do about dinner? I'm getting hungry."

So I smiled, finished the beer and said, "Why do you think I've got swim trunks on? There's a supermarket of seafood under us, dear."

I had found a locker onboard filled with snorkeling gear. With mask and fins, I jumped overboard into what I hoped was water not more than 15 or 20 feet deep.

And what I found was in fact the seafood supermarket I had hoped would be there. Five dives later and after some on-deck grilling time, Sandy and I were feasting on Caribbean lobster tails and a half dozen of the biggest shrimp we had ever seen. There were also a couple of nice red snappers I had managed to spear. They filleted out nicely and the meat tasted sweat and firm.

Our hunger satiated, we lounged on the deck, finishing two bottles of nice California chardonnay. We became mesmerized by millions of stars lighting up a clear sky, a sight you don't see in or near a city.

It took us an hour or so after going into the main cabin to get to sleep, but we enjoyed the time. Bright daylight woke us and we were greeted by two men sitting on our boat's deck.

One of the men, dark skinned, short, heavy-set, and

smiling broadly exposing big yellow teeth, held what I recognized as an AK-47. The other man, fair skinned and blond hair cut short in a military style, held a big semi-auto pistol.

"Good morning," the blond haired guy said brightly. "It's a beautiful day and if you play this wrong it will be your last day."

****

So even there in the middle of nowhere, we couldn't get away from danger and the black shroud of The Grim Reaper.

"Who the hell are you?" I asked rather stupidly. After all, it really doesn't matter who it is holds the guns, now does it?

"I'm the guy who needs your boat," the blond guy answered.

"But it's not our boat," Sandy said. I winced when she said it, but what the hell. "It's a rental," she said, I guess hoping that would make a difference.

"OK," I said and took a step forward which didn't make either of the men happy. The AK-47 was leveled at me and the big semi-auto was pointed right at my head.

"Wait a minute," I said. "I just want to find out what's going on and maybe we can deal our way out of this."

"Deal?" he answered. "What deal? The best you two can hope for is to still be alive ten minutes from now. I told you I want your boat."

"OK," I said. "So take it. We can't stop you. But tell us what we have to do to keep you from killing us."

Well," he said glancing at a big, gaudy, gold and diamond encrusted wrist watch. "I've got three hours to wait. The first thing you can do is have the pretty lady go below and whip up some breakfast. I haven't eaten yet today."

Sandy spoke up and said, "We don't have any food on board."

"Bullshit!" he said. "You folks aren't going to be doing some kind of Hindu fast out here."

"We were going to pull into a port today to stock up," I said. "We ate what we pulled from the ocean last night. We've got coffee, but that's all."

"OK," he said. "I could use some coffee and I'm sure my buddy Jose here would like some, too"

"Usted quiere el café, Jose?" he asked the man holding the rifle.

"Sí, el café es bueno" the little fat guy said smiling broadly.

"Yeah," the blond guy said. "Jose's good with a gun and not much else. But he's easy to please. So anyway, lady," he said. "Go below and whip up a pot of coffee."

I nodded to Sandy and she took the four steps down into the cabin and started on the coffee. I eased over to the ship's rail where a rope was tied and I looked down. An inflatable boat with a big outboard motor was tied up.

I leaned against the rail and watched the two men light cigarettes and talk back and forth in Spanish. I caught a word or two but I am barely fluent in English.

Talking always seemed to be the right thing to do, so I said, "Who are you guys, anyway?"

The blond guy answered, "No names. I hate to kill people I know. So it's gonna be easier to shoot the two of you if I don't know who you are. And if by chance you make it through the day, I don't want you knowing who the hell I am, either."

The two men spoke quietly in Spanish again until Sandy brought a glass pot of coffee and four large mugs onto the deck. We each drank the hot coffee, Sandy and I waiting near the cabin's entrance, as far from the two gunmen as we could get.

After about ten minutes, the blond haired guy said, "OK. We might as well get going. We'll be early but what the hell."

"Early for what?" I asked.

"For our appointment," he answered snidely. "Pull up the anchors and get the engines going."

"We don't have much fuel," I said as I pulled up the rear anchor and started forward to that anchor.

"Don't matter," he answered. "We'll get fuel when we get there. You know how to navigate?"

I said, "Not really, but the boat's equipped with a computer navigation system."

"Great," he said, smiling. "We're headed for 25.49 latitude and 77.82 longitude. Do what you need to do to get us there. Shouldn't take too long but if we're not there in two hours exactly . . . I'll have Jose here kill you both."

So off we went, towing the little inflatable behind us, but where the hell were we going? I started the engines and plugged the GPS coordinates into the computer. I thought for a moment that maybe I should send an email via satellite to someone and get some help. But I looked up and found what's his name looking at me from the doorway to the cabin, holding his semi-auto and shaking his head.

"Just enter the coordinates. Don't do anything stupid, OK?" he said.

Between Jose and his buddy the coffee was gone in short notice. Sandy made some more and while it was brewing she had the idea that maybe giving the two our booze would be a good idea. If they were to get drunk, maybe – she thought – she and I could take their weapons and head for the closest port and help.

She came up the steps carrying a liter bottle of vodka and offered it to the two.

"We don't have any food, but maybe you'd enjoy a drink? Just to pass the time," she said brightly.

Jose grinned happily and lunged for the bottle but his

English speaking buddy grabbed his arm and shook his head.

"We need to stay sober," he said. "But after this is all over, maybe you and me can party and get drunk," he said, leering at Sandy.

"Yeah," she said carrying the bottle back down into the cabin. "I don't think so."

She locked herself in the forward bedroom, determined to stay there as long as she could. That was a good idea, I thought.

I kept a close eye on the fuel gauges and on the depth finder as we were in fairly shallow waters. We didn't have a long distance to go so I ran the two big engines on slow revs, hoping to conserve some diesel fuel.

It was getting hot and I filled up on water, noticing that neither gunman drank anything but uncounted mugs of hot coffee. That was good, I knew, because soon they would be feeling dehydrated, dizzy, and hopefully sick as they sat out in the sun on the open deck.

But in less than the two hours I was given we arrived at the coordinates and I stopped the engines.

"OK," the guy said as he felt the boat slow to a stop. "Drop the anchor off . . . what the hell do you call it? The front?"

The anchor took all the chain from the boat before touching bottom. As the chain played out I looked off to the southern horizon and saw a dark shadow approaching. As it got closer I saw it was a beaten up, battered and rusty old tub of a ship, maybe 80 or 90 feet in length.

Jose and his good buddy looked up, saw it and stood.

"OK," Jose's friend said. "Get down below with the woman, keep your mouth shut and you might just live through this. There are about a dozen really bad Colombians on that wreck and they'll cut you up and eat you for lunch. Then they'll party hardy with your lady."

THE LINE

So it was a drug deal. I talked Sandy into unlocking the door to the forward bedroom and joined her there, locking the door behind me.

Out on the deck I could hear the conversation through the open air vent in the ceiling of the cabin:

"Hey Johnny!" someone called out loudly. The voice had a Spanish accent attached to it. I heard what sounded like someone jumping onto the open deck. So the man with the gun was called Johnny. At least I learned something.

"Where'd you get this boat?" the same accented voice asked. "What happened to that rat bucket you usually take?"

"Damn engine trouble," Johnny answered. "Me and Jose had to hijack this one. Pretty nice boat, though. I may keep it."

"Hey, Johnny. You know that ain't smart. This boat, she can be traced. Sink it when the business is done."

"Yeah," Johnny said. "You're probably right. Nice boat though. Got a really cool computer GPS system."

"Too bad. You dump the people had the boat?"

"No, not yet," Johnny answered.

"What you mean! You gotta dump'em. You know that. They can talk."

"And if I had, they're damn bodies would be floating out there. They'd be found and ID'ed and the Feds would eventually trace the boat," Johnny said. "No, I'm gonna bury'em on this little sandy atoll I know about," he said. "It'll be a thousand damn years before anybody finds'em."

"You mean you got people on board here?"

"They're locked up below," Johnny answered. "My man Jose will kill them if they stick their heads out."

"That ain't so good," The accented guy said. "You better kill'em now, yes?"

"No, I don't think so," Johnny answered.

I could hear the tension between the two men without having to see them. These were drug smugglers and I was fully aware of the kind of people they were. Killing was just part of the business and if killing assured big profits, they didn't particularly care who had to die.

"I got a use for them," he said. "After we get done here, I need someone to navigate the damn boat. It's computer controlled and way above my head."

"Bullshit," the accent answered.

"Don't push me, Santo," Johnny answered. I had another name . . . if I lived long enough to use it.

There was a moment or two of silence out on the deck. I could imagine the two men staring at each other, weighing the possibilities, figuring the odds.

Then Santo broke the silence and said, "OK. It's your nuts that could be hangin' in the wind, yes? Let's get business done. You got the money?"

"You know better than that," Johnny said. "Like it's always been, the cash is gonna' be wire transferred as soon as I radio in. And if I don't radio in my people are gonna' find you . . . your wife . . . your kids . . . your mama . . . your friggin' dog. And if your kids don't have a dog, they'll buy a dog for them and then kill it."

"Hey! No problem, me amigo," Santo said.

There was very little conversation after that. Sandy and I listened carefully. It sounded like more people than just Johnny, Jose and Santo were transferring cargo — we agreed it had to be drugs — from the cargo ship to the Good

Luck. The name of our motor cruiser didn't do anything good for our luck.

I glanced at my Rolex and then did the same again. It took about forty minutes to move the drugs onto our little boat.

We whispered our thoughts to each other.

"What do you think will happen now," Sandy asked.

"Haven't the foggiest my dear," I answered. I didn't tell her that I really believed the odds were no better than 50 - 50 that Johnny and Jose would not kill us right then and there. We were witnesses after all and witnesses were bad news for people in their business.

"Isn't there something we can do?" Sandy asked. "How about offering them some money?"

"That was my thought, too," I said. "How much?"

"Does that matter? Whatever they want," Sandy said.

"And if they want it they have to let us live long enough to get to a bank," I said, trying to encourage her a little.

"Do you really believe Johnny's gonna bury us like he said," She asked.

"I can't say he doesn't want to. These guys are real nasty bastards. And he can't leave any witnesses behind."

"And how does that affect buying him off? If he takes our money, won't he be leaving witnesses behind?" Sandy suggested.

Right away I knew I shouldn't have said what I said about leaving witnesses behind. What I wasn't telling her was that when it was just the two of us and Jose and Johnny, when we were close enough to some land, anywhere, I was going to toss Sandy overboard and try as best as I could to hold the two of them off while she swam away.

I would wait for the right time, if they didn't kill us right away. Then Johnny knocked on the cabin's door and said, "OK you two. You can come out now. The bad guys are gone."

We hesitated but we did unlock the door and stepped out. Johnny was in the galley putting sliced ham and cheese on a couple slices of bread.

"Where did you get the food at?" Sandy asked without hiding any of her surprise.

"Oh, we got food," Johnny said. "The fridge's stocked . . . We even got some steaks for dinner tonight. And both tanks are topped off with diesel. We're all set, ain't we? Those Colombians are mighty nice guys and very generous. 'Course I had to pay for it."

The food was a good idea, of course. And we certainly needed the diesel, but what we didn't need was a cabin well stocked with plastic wrapped bricks of some kind of illegal drugs. I took a quick count and came up with about 70 or 75 in the cabin and after going up on deck, I counted another 100 or more out there.

I figured it would just make things worse if I said anything about the cargo we now carried, but Sandy and I really needed some food.

"How about a couple of the sandwiches for us?" I asked.

"Hey! Help yourselves! There's plenty for everybody."

As we started to make up sandwiches Jose stepped down into the cabin.

"Hey," he said in good English. "Make one of those for me, will you? And how about a cold beer while you're at it?"

"You speak English!" Sandy said. I thought . . ."

"Of course I speak English. What'd you think?" Jose answered.

"I thought you couldn't speak English, Jose," I said.

"The name's not Jose," Johnny said. "This is Henry Lubbock."

"What . . . Henry . . . What" I stammered.

"Yeah, that's right," Jose/Henry said. "And don't call me Hank. I don't like to be called Hank."

"I don't get it," Sandy said. "What the hell's going on here?"

"I really think," I said, "that you need to tell us what's happening here."

"OK," Johnny said. "Henry here and me, we're D.E.A."

Sandy looked questioningly at both them and me so I interjected proudly and knowingly, "That's Drug Enforcement Administration. If he's not lying, then they're Feds."

"Oh, we're not lying," Henry said.

"But I thought you were some kind of South American drug killer or something," Sandy said.

"South American? I was born in East L.A., lady. I'm as American as you are. My mother's from Peru, my Dad, he's from Mississippi. I was even in the Marines, lady. I love my friggin' Country. And Mickey here, he loves it, too."

"Mickey? I heard that guy call you Johnny," I said.

"That's what those bastards know me as," Mickey/Johnny said. "I got to keep a . . . what'ya call it? . . . nom de plume or something like that. You see," he went on, "me and Henry, we rip off drug dealers."

"But you said you were D.E.A.," I said.

"Yeah, well, we're on contract with the D.E.A. We get paid when we bust a deal. We don't get a paycheck," Henry answered.

"So we're really not in any danger?" Sandy asked. "You're not really going to kill us?"

"Of course not," Mickey answered. "Well, maybe if you screw things up, we might have to slit your damn throats."

After a few seconds of stunned silence, both Mickey and Henry broke out in laughter.

"Just kidding," Henry said. "By the way, since you know who we are, who the hell are you?

"I'm Morgan Crew," I said. "This is Sandy Crew, my wife."

"Wait a minute," Henry said. "Are you that guy that's always in the news? That rich guy?"

"I don't know who you're reading about," I answered. "I've got a few bucks set aside if that means anything to you. And I've got a wolf pack of big time lawyers who will hunt you down if anything happens to us."

"Are you threatening us, Mr. Crew?" Henry asked.

"I don't make threats," I answered. "I do make promises that I never break."

I was feeling a little bit more assured and brave now that I knew these guys weren't drug dealer-killers. And Sandy was feeling the same. She had been withdrawn and quiet all this time, staying in the background. I knew she was scared but until then there was little I could do about it. Now I was feeling a little bit more confident and maybe that confidence would find its way into Sandy.

"OK, OK," she said, stepping from behind me. "I've heard this tossing of threats back and forth before. Everybody stop it and let's get down to business.

"You want us to take you somewhere," she went on. "Since we're being honest with each other, how about telling us where we're going?"

"Sure," Mickey said and smiled at her. "Since we're being honest . . . as you say. We're going to meet another boat. This one is manned by a bunch of Cubans out of Miami. And they're *really* bad guys."

THE SINKER

And so we cruised on into the afternoon. Mickey said to keep a course of 8 degrees west of north and to slow the engines, which I did without asking why.

It was hot as the afternoon dragged on and there was only a slight breeze. Sandy and I decided to stay below, lounging among the bricks of drugs and sipping on a couple of cold vodka martinis. The food left for us by the Colombians was good but the booze was better.

The main cabin was lined with windows and I traded off looking out of them with checking the computer GPS and depth finder. I almost wanted to run the Good Luck onto a sand bar, but I wasn't sure what that would do for us.

Sandy was deep in thought and after awhile said, "Do you think these guys are telling us the truth? Do you really think they're D.E.A. Agents?"

As I understand it," I answered. "Mickey and Henry are contract agents, which means they're like mercenaries. They do things for the D.E.A. and get paid for what they do.

"It also means they're not necessarily pure souls," I went on. "I mean, they work independently, without anyone overseeing what they do. I've heard stories about guys like these. They're basically bad guys working for the good guys and they don't mind doing what the bad guys do . . . like killing when they feel it necessary. I wouldn't trust any of them."

"When they do what they're going to do today," Sandy asked. "Do you think they'll actually let us go . . . alive I mean?"

I didn't want her to worry any more than she was already worrying, so I didn't tell her what I was really thinking.

"I guess so," I lied. "I mean, I don't think they have any reason to hurt us. Look at it this way. Assume their boat really had engine trouble, like Mickey said back there. They had to have a boat and we were the closest boat, so they hijacked ours. If they hadn't, they wouldn't have been able to do whatever it is they're going to be paid for doing. We might even be good witnesses that they did the job . . . whatever that is . . . and should be paid for it."

What I really felt and was fighting to not believe, was that it was still only 50 – 50 at best that we would walk away, unless we could gain control of the situation. But how do we do that?

Sandy nodded in agreement and said, "Yes, I suppose so. But I'd feel a lot better if we had a gun, too."

I poured another martini for each of us and after starting it I could feel the effects beginning. That was always good but right then I knew I needed a clear head. So I grabbed Sandy's glass and along with mine, poured both down the sink.

"What's that for," Sandy asked?

"Look," I said, "We have to stay straight. We might still be in trouble."

"You're thinking of a way to get their guns, aren't you?" she asked, grinning broadly.

Sandy could always read my mind, ever since we first met way back in San Marcos. Sandy is smart, quick, and when necessary, she can be tough. I had to count on that now, if for no other reason than to use everything we had together to keep her from harm.

"Yes," I said. "I really would like to get my hands on

one or both of their guns. I'd feel better if we were in charge."

"OK. And how do we do that? I mean, I can probably kick the crap out of one of them, but not both of them," Sandy said laughing.

"So far," I said, "they haven't been separated. If we could figure out some way to get them apart . . . maybe . . ."

"Maybe what?" Sandy asked. "You think you can take one of them if the other isn't around?"

"Hell, not bare handed," I said. "I'm thinking if I could get behind one of them and smack them over the head with something . . ."

"And then what would you do with the other one?"

I didn't have an answer for that.

"You're saying you'd shoot the other one? I doubt either one would lose a Mexican stand-off against you. And remember, they are supposed to be working for the D.E.A."

"Yeah," I said. "That's the other thing. Let's say their telling us the truth and they really are on a D.E.A. contract. Why are they sitting up there still holding their guns? Why not be down here enjoying a few drinks and our company?"

"You're saying what I think you're saying?" Sandy asked.

"I'm saying quite plainly that we aren't out of the swamp yet and there are still a couple of alligators chomping on our asses."

We were quiet for awhile. I stood at the sink in the galley, looking through the window there and watching a small island go by. It was miniscule, very white sand and sported two raggedy palm trees that needed a good drink of water. I wondered if that was the island Mickey was talking about. The one where he said he would bury us.

My thoughts were interrupted by Henry who walked down the five steps into the cabin.

"We're there," he said. "Mickey says to stop the boat and drop anchor. We'll wait here."

****

So I climbed up to the flying bridge and stopped the engines. I made my way forward and dropped the bow anchor. That was a mistake because the boat was still moving and the anchor chain dragged the bottom, swinging under the boat and scratching the fiberglass hull. The boat swung around and finally came to a stop.

When I looked back at the open deck both Henry and Mickey were laughing.

"Hey," Mickey said. "You ain't such a good ship's captain after all."

Making my way back to the open deck I noticed another boat, this one long and sleek, painted a bright red, coming towards us very fast. It was kicking up a big wake and bouncing even on the calm Caribbean waters.

From the deck, standing too near to Mickey and Henry, I saw Sandy out of the corner of my eye. I motioned to her to go back into the forward sleeping cabin.

Turning to the two men I said, "Look, you guys have business. I'm going back into the forward bedroom. Is that OK?"

"Yeah," Henry said. "That's best. These guys are pretty bad and they shouldn't see you."

From inside the locked room Sandy and I heard a lot of talk in Spanish. We only made out a word or two, but the conversation sounded friendly enough. There was a lot of movement and conversation as we assumed the drugs were being moved from the Good Luck onto the Cuban's boat.

"What the hell's happening?" Sandy said.

"I really don't know," I answered. "I guess this is all part of the operation the D.E.A. has planned."

"What kind of plan is it to buy drugs and turn everything over to some Cubans? And what are they going to do with it? Are they going to smuggle it into the United States?"

"Sandy," I said. "I really don't know. All I know is we're still alive and well. There's got to be a reason for that. I mean, they don't need me to drive this damn boat. All they have to do is turn off the computer and sit up on the flying bridge and steer the boat. Anybody can do that."

"So, why?" Sandy wondered. "Maybe they really are D.E.A. people and we're really not in danger? Maybe they really just needed a boat, like they said."

"Sandy my dear," I said. "I just hope you're right. I have this gut feeling . . . and that damn little voice in the back of my head is screaming again . . . things just aren't like they're supposed to be."

All my life I have found myself in one kind of trouble or another. Most of the time it was because I was expected to help someone out of trouble by getting myself into trouble. Whatever the cause I have this little voice in the back of my head that warns me of trouble brewing. Right then I hear it screaming, "GET OUT! GET OUT! RUN AWAY!"

I've ignored that little voice . . . at least most of the time . . . and every time I do I wind up getting into deep, deep trouble. That little voice was screaming as loud as I've ever heard it but there was little I could do about it.

And so we waited. Time slipped by slowly but eventually the sounds up on deck came to an end and we heard the Cuban's big boat rev up and speed off.

"OK," Mickey called down to us. "It's safe now, you can come on out. It's time to celebrate."

When we unlocked and opened the door we joined Henry and Mickey in the main cabin. They were at the small table near the galley counting cash out of a large suitcase.

"How much did you get?" Sandy asked.

"A million bucks, lady! Ain't that great! And nobody got killed!" Henry said.

"So you'll now turn that into the D.E.A.? You get

some kind of reward?" I asked.

"Yeah, we get a fifteen percent reward.   That's $150,000! Our biggest pay day yet," Mickey answered.

"And the Cubans with all the drugs," Sandy asked. "What happens to them?"

"They're on their way to Miami. A dozen Feds are waiting for them," Henry said.

"So anyway," Mickey said. "We're going to stay here tonight and drink up all that booze you folks were kind enough to supply. And I hope you'll join us."

We agreed rather than argue with the man with the gun. Sandy and I went down into the galley and made up a whole platter of sandwiches, using up the last of the ham and deep yellow cheddar cheese. While we were hard at work Mickey and Henry went up to the sun drenched deck.

We had brought six bottles of good wine onboard and none had been opened yet. I whispered to Sandy, "Let them drink the hard stuff. We should stick to the wine and go easy on that."

She nodded agreement and I carried the tray of sandwiches up to the deck while Sandy carried what was left of the liter of vodka and the unopened liter of bourbon. Under her arm was a bottle of good California Cabernet for her and me.

"Hey! That looks great," Mickey said as he grabbed a couple of sandwiches and swallowed them in three or four mouthfuls. Henry reached for the vodka.

A little over an hour later the sun was low in the western sky and Henry was plastered. Mickey had been drinking but not as hard and as fast as Henry.

Henry began to sing a sad sounding song in Spanish and stumbled toward the rail to sit on a padded bench. Sandy and I were sitting on the other side of the open deck. Mickey eased towards us, put his finger to his lips and bent towards us.

"Look," he said in a whisper. "You two have to get off

the boat. Henry there doesn't want you around. He wants to keep the cash for himself and he doesn't want any witnesses. I been trying to talk him out of it, but once he gets his mind made up there's no changing it.

"Use the inflatable and get the hell outta' here," he said. "There's enough gas to get you to The Bahamas. Henry's drunk enough so he won't notice you're gone until you're far enough away."

It didn't take much for Sandy and me to agree that Mickey had a great idea. We stepped as quietly as we could to the inflatable that Mickey and Henry had taken to the Good Luck, still tied to the aft. We eased our way down and Mickey untied the rope holding the little boat.

I guessed that the sound of the big outboard on the inflatable would draw Henry's attention, but there was nothing I could do about that.

There was a wheel and small control board at the front of the boat. I saw a key and a button that looked like a starter. The outboard roared to life and I pushed the throttle full forward. The little boat almost jumped out of the water but we were on our way.

Within seconds we heard a gunshot and we both turned in time to see Henry standing at the rail, his face blown away by the gunshot to the back of his head. He fell forward into the blue Caribbean Sea.

I slowed the boat but Sandy said, "What the hell are you doing! Get us the hell outta' here!"

As she said that, the engines on the Good Luck started, and Mickey, up on the flying bridge, turned the wheel. We watched as he and our rented boat cruised away from us.

THE CATCH

Late afternoon turned into evening and evening turned into night. Having watched the setting sun, I knew basically what direction east was and I kept the boat on that heading as best I could.

West would mean going ashore in Cuba and we didn't need to do that. I doubted that my attorneys would have much pull there and I'd heard all about their prisons. So east was where I needed to take us.

I knew there were a lot of islands in the Bahamas chain. Most were uninhabited but if we were lucky we would run into an island with people on it or maybe a fishing boat . . . anything.

Midnight passed and although we could count thousands of stars overhead, we didn't see anything like land in front of us.

It was about a quarter to two in the morning that the engine started sputtering and soon died. We were out of gas and there was nothing within sight . . . anywhere.

The sun rose and the air started to heat up. We were drifting with a slight breeze that was . . . I think . . . pushing us west instead of east.

"What are we going to do, Morgan?" Sandy asked.

Again I didn't tell her what was really on my mind. I said, "Look, we have to be in some kind of major shipping route. Cuba is to the west and the Bahamas are to the east. Ships have to pass through this area. We'll probably get picked up sometime today."

What I really thought was that we were in a miniscule little boat in the middle of a pretty big body of water. Chances were a whole lot better than even that a dozen ships could pass by east and west, miles away from us, without ever seeing our little rubber boat.

The day wore on and the sun got hotter by the hour. We had no water and no shade. Sandy wanted to get into the water to cool off.

"I'm not sure that's a really good idea," I said. "When you get out you be soaked with salt water. That and the sun will be really tough on your skin. Plus, there are sharks all over the place here. "

Sandy was dressed in cotton shorts and a light blouse. I was dressed in light weight slacks and a golf shirt. "Get undressed," Sandy said.

"Now is not the time, dear," I said.

"Not that you idiot. Get the clothes wet and then cover what we can with them, heads first. The evaporating water will cool us off a little."

She was right, of course, as she always is. It did help and throughout the heat of the day we kept the clothing wet. But as the sun was setting the air cooled off and a breeze came up from the east, stronger than we had seen in the past few days.

We huddled down in the bottom of the boat, holding each other tightly to keep as warm as we could. The sea got choppy at first then the swells rose and we hoped we could ride it out.

Rain started and got heavier. "I wish we had something to catch the rain in," Sandy said. "It would make good drinking water for tomorrow."

The rain started to fill the boat but my hopes at having something to drink later were dashed when waves started breaking over the inflated walls of the little boat, fouling the rain water.

"Open your mouth," I told Sandy. "Drink in what you can. It may be all we're going to get for awhile."

Although the sea produced waves maybe six or eight feet high, the little inflatable held its own. It was a long and very frightening night but we made it through to sunrise and calm seas once again. We were drenched and cold but we knew the sun would start on us again soon.

It took a long time but we managed to bail most of the water out of the boat by hand. The rain water we managed to drink in help a lot but we knew it wouldn't last forever.

As we were bailing we felt a bump against the boat, then another and then more. I looked over the side and found we were surrounded by sharks that were testing the strange thing in their water to see if it were edible.

It was well past noon and we were huddled at the edge of the boat, keeping our clothing wet again when Sandy heard it before I did.

"What's that?" she asked.

"What?"

"I hear a boat . . . a motor."

I quickly scanned the horizon and at first didn't see anything. The sun was deadly bright and lit up the water, reflecting back to my burning eyes. But then I saw it, a small black thing getting bigger as it got closer to us.

Sandy stood and began to yell and wave her blouse over her head. I joined her, waving and yelling as loud as my dry throat would allow.

Whoever was on the boat saw us and turned to come straight at us.

Sandy stopped yelling, slipped on her shorts and blouse and said, "You don't think they're more drug dealers, do you?"

"I hope not. Do we have a choice?" I answered.

As it turned out it wasn't a boat full of killers, it was a

boat full of Bahamian fishermen. They saw us and picked us up and gave us water and beer and food we didn't recognize but ate with hungered delight. Communication between us was difficult but they understood without having been told that we had been stranded and they took us back to their home island.

The island was sandy and rocky and spotted with tall palms. The beach was mainly small stones but there was a stream flowing from the interior of the island into the majestically clear sea lapping onto the beach. A dozen small huts, thatch roofed and raised on wooden stilts in case of storm tossed high tides, were lined up all facing the sea.

There was a lively – to say the least – party thrown for us that evening; the beer and conch and fish flowed like water. Several times we were offered what smelled suspiciously like marijuana. We declined as graciously as we could.

The people were poor, dressed in little more than ragged shirts and pants, but they were generous with what they had.

Sandy and I ate, drank, danced and sang with them and in the morning a Bahamian Coast Guard boat picked us up. We guessed that someone on the small island had a radio, but we didn't ask. The idea of getting into Nassau was all we could think about.

It was early evening when we stepped off the boat in Nassau. We found a mediocre hotel near the harbor and checked in, showered and fell onto the lumpy bed in pure exhaustion.

In the morning we drank coffee from the in-room coffee maker and started for the American Consulate.

Inside Sandy began to get frustrated at being shuffled off between various offices. We saw everyone from the Assistant to the Administrative Assistant of the Assistant Consul all the way up to the Secretary for American Tourism and a couple of dozen meaningless people in between,

Finally, when she had had enough, as we were walking down a hallway, she turned and grabbed a Marine Guard by the collar. If he hadn't been so surprised he probably would have thrown her onto the floor.

But he didn't and she said, looking up at the face on his 6'5" frame, "Who the hell do we see about being kidnapped by God Damn drug smugglers!"

"Try the Drug Enforcement Administration, lady," he said.

"Where the hell is that?" she said.

"Third floor, number 341, Miss. Now let go of me or you won't get to see anybody but the inside of a jail cell," the Marine said.

Sandy let go of the Marine, turned and smiled at me with a wink of her gorgeous eye.

"Let's go Morgan," she said. "Third floor, 341." She was feeling quite good about herself and I was feeling quite good about her, too.

We found room 341 and walked in. Four desks with computer screens and keyboards on each all but filled the small room. A line of filing cabinets ran along one wall. On the wall opposite the doorway was a wall of windows looking out over four blocks of buildings to the harbor. But there were no people in the office.

"Hello!" I called out. "Is anybody here?"

No one answered so Sandy suggested, "Could they be out for lunch?"

I checked my Rolex and found it was five minutes past ten in the morning.

"I doubt it," I said. "Maybe early morning cocktails, but not lunch."

Then a door opened in a back corner of the office and a young man walked through. He was dressed in stained tan shorts and a rumpled Caribbean flowered shirt open at the color. His feet pulled battered sandals across the floor. He was unshaven, by the looks of it for several days at least.

His hair needed a brushing at least, a good washing would have been better. He was reading whatever a crumpled manila folder held.

He was half way into the office before he realized we were standing in the doorway.

"Oh, sorry," he said. "Who'd you want to see?"

"I don't know," Sandy said. "Is this the D.E.A. or what?"

"Yeah, I guess," he said as he sat at a desk. "What'ya want?"

"Look," I said walking towards him. "Stop the crap. We want to see someone. We want to report a kidnapping and theft."

"Ok," he said. "Go try the cops. They're pretty good at that sort of thing."

Sandy ran to his desk and pushed the guy backwards out of his chair. I can always count on Sandy to get people's attention when needed.

She stood over him and growled, "We were kidnapped by drug dealers, our lives were threatened, our boat was stolen, and we witnessed a murder and a massive drug exchange for money. Now if you're more than a coffee fetcher around here, you'll hear us out and then do something about it."

From behind us, in the doorway, someone yelled, "Hold it! Get your hands over your heads! Move! Now!"

I turned slowly and Sandy spun around. Two men were in the doorway holding handguns in a very professional and threatening manner.

"Alright, wait a minute," I said holding my arms sort of half way over my head. "We're just trying to find someone to talk to, that's all. This guy was being a jerk," I said pointing at the young man still on the floor.

"That jerk is my son," the older of the two men said. They were dressed in light weight business suits, dark in color, white shirts and striped ties.

I explained who we were and what we had been through as quickly as I could, leaving out all the details. They seemed to believe us, holstered their guns and told us to sit at one of the desks.

We learned that the young man Sandy was about to beat the crap out of was the son of Agent Mathew Henson. He had just arrived from having been kicked out of college for carrying a strong 0.75 GPA.

Anyway, we sat at the desk across from Agent Henson and his partner Agent Stan Viteli and told them our story in great detail.

Henson and Viteli looked at each other, shook their heads and Viteli said, "You mean this guy Mickey killed this guy Henry?

"Yes, like we said," Sandy told him. "He said he was a D.E.A. contract agent. That can't be true."

The two men looked at each other again and then Henson said, "Sounds like The Mouth."

Viteli nodded and I said, "Wait a minute . . . You're saying this guy is Mickey the Mouth! You've got to be kidding."

"Some people started calling him Mickey Mouth as a joke. He killed a couple of them and the joke ended.

"His real name is Tony Martinelli, Henson explained. "He's a former NYPD Detective. He got suspended a few years ago for beating the crap out of his Lieutenant. He never came back to work . . . disappeared. Since then he's been ripping off South American drug smugglers. He works for us occasionally, but mainly he works for himself.

"He thinks he can talk his way into and out of everything, so he got the nickname The Mouth. Lately he's been doing a lot of killing. You say he was with someone called Henry? A Latino who claimed to be from L.A.? That sounds like Luis LaManna.

"He was a Marine, like he told you," Henson continued. "He was arrested in Iraq for murdering a few dozen civilians. He escaped and he's been on the run since. He's dead now, huh?"

Sandy and I were quiet for a minute or two, drinking it all in. Then I asked, "So, this Tony Martinelli actually got away with a million dollars?"

"Looks that way," Viteli said.

A phone rang and Henson's son picked it up, spoke a few words, and then said, "You Morgan Crew?"

"Yes, that's me," I answered.

"Call's for you," he said.

"Who knows we're here?" Sandy asked.

"Nobody," I said and picked up a nearby phone.

"Morgan, old buddy . . . It's me, Tony Martinelli. How you doing?"

I motioned to Sandy to pick up a phone, and then said, "How the hell did you know I'd be here?"

"Hell, I'm not exactly dumb, you know," he said. "I figured it would take just about this much time for you to be found, for you to get to Nassau and then, of course, I figured you'd go right to the D.E.A. Good guess, huh?"

"Where are you?" I asked and motioned to Henson and Viteli to pick up phones.

"I'm on a sunny beach somewhere," he answered. "I've got this beautiful babe on my right and a bucket of beer on ice on my left. Pretty good, huh?"

"You intended all alone to keep all that money, then?" Sandy asked.

"Of course," he said. "If I really had done all that for the Feds I would have wound up with a few thousand."

"But what about Luis LaManna?" I asked. "Did you have to kill him?"

"Luis was a crazy killer. A maniac. I did everyone a favor when I blew his brains out. Hell, he's so bad I'll bet even the sharks are leaving him alone. And besides . . . a million dollars is twice as much as half a million if I had to split it with him."

We were all silent for what seemed an eternity. Then Tony said, "Hey Mr. and Mrs. Crew. Have a good life." The line went dead

The End

SUMMER KILL

THE HOOK

We were relaxing on the upper level of our deck at our home in the hills of San Marcos, California, above the harbor. Sandy was stretched out on a chaise, dressed in her new bikini, in the shade of a tall pine to relieve the heat of the hot August afternoon. I was sitting in the full sun, lathered well with sun tan lotion, trying to get a tan so that people wouldn't mistake me for the Pillsbury Dough Boy.

The month of May – and our time in the Caribbean – had come and gone with Sandy and me still alive. We had spent the month of June in a rented Mercedes driving interminably slow via every off-the-beaten-track road we could find back to San Marcos.

July 4th was celebrated with a Bar-B-Que at our house. A couple dozen friends showed up, and a few people we didn't know joined them. That evening we all crowded on the tri-level deck of our house and watched the fireworks hosted by the City as they lit the sky above the harbor.

Without speaking a word to each other, we stood looking down at the familiar harbor and thought of old friends, Cap'n Nick and Franco Morelli.

That night we ate our fill of hamburgers and hot dogs and corn on the cob and everything else that we had laid out for the occasion. The beer and wine helped to fog the memories.

My friend from my college years, Lt. Bob Sommers of the San Marcos Police Department, was the last to arrive. As was his habit, he walked straight for the food. He passed by the beer and threw down what he imagined were glasses of very expensive wine. The wine wasn't all that expensive, by the way.

I think everyone had a good time and around midnight people started to leave. Bob Sommers was still there when everyone else had left. Sandy and I sat in chairs near him as he drank yet another glass of red wine.

It had been apparent from the time Bob walked through the front door that something was troubling him. Bob, although he was a good cop and good detective, he tended to wear his emotions on his sleeve.

Sandy spoke first. "Bob. What's wrong? You look like someone died."

"How'd you know that?" he asked, his words slurred slightly by all the wine he had thrown down.

"Know what?' I asked.

"Damn it, Morgan," he said. "How'd you find out? No one is supposed to know."

"Bob, please," Sandy said. "I don't know what you're talking about."

"Nobody was supposed to know, yet," he said. "We haven't even made a press release."

"Bob," I said. "Please, what the hell are you talking about?"

"The murders," he said as if we were supposed to know. "You mean you don't know?"

"What murders?" Sandy asked.

Bob sat up in his chair, took another mouthful of wine, straightened his back, and then said, "I guess I might as well tell you. I mean that's what I had in mind anyway. There's been three murders in the last six weeks," he said. "Prostitutes out of North Harbor. They were all stabbed . . . multiple times . . . and their throats were slashed. Really bloody. They were all done the same."

North Harbor is a decrepit and derelict section of San Marcos. Back in the 1920s and 30s it was a nice, middle class neighborhood where the fishermen and working class lived with their families. Today it is populated by the dregs of San Marcos society; the drunks, the drug addicts, the prostitutes. Cheap bars that sport topless and nude dancers are everywhere. Drugs of any kind are easy to find.

"That doesn't surprise me," I said. "I mean . . . prostitutes live a dangerous life."

"Morgan Crew!" Sandy snapped. "They *are* people after all. Have a little compassion!"

"OK," I said. "I'll give it a try."

Then I turned to Bob and asked, "And just what does this have to do with us?"

"I need you to use that damn Crew family influence of yours for me," he said.

"Bob," I said. "Stop being obtuse and tell me what you want."

"What the hell's obtuse?" he asked in a semi-drunken slur.

"You know damn well what obtuse is, Bob." I said. "You went through college with me. You aren't obtuse but you're acting very obtuse right know. Cut the crap and get to the point."

"OK," he started. "The FBI came to town this morning. They want to take over the case. They said I have to get out of it. They wouldn't tell me why. I need you to phone whoever you have to and find out why the FBI would be interested in the murders of prostitutes."

I looked at Sandy and she looked at me. I could almost hear her thinking, "Not again, Morgan."

"Bob," I said. "How am I supposed to find that out?"

"You've done stuff like that for other people," he said. "Why not for me? I'm supposed to be your friend."

He pushed himself out of his chair and stumbled toward the table holding the wine. Most of the bottles were empty, but he found a couple with dregs and a couple with an ounce or two of wine. He emptied all of these into his glass, mixing a half dozen different wines, red and white, together.

While he was at the table Sandy whispered to me, "Morgan. Let's not get involved in this. Let's just enjoy the weather. Tell you what . . . I'll even take you out fishing and spend more time at the Country Club with you. How about that?"

"He's my friend, Sandy," I said. "I can't just turn him away. What harm can a few phone calls make?"

Bob made his uneasy way back to us and fell into his chair. He had had way too much to drink. There was no way he could drive himself down the winding roads back to Downtown.

"Alright, Bob," I said. "First you're going to spend the night here . . . Sleep it off. Then we're going to have a big breakfast in the morning . . . With lots of strong coffee. After that the three of us are going to talk and we'll see if I'm going to make those phone calls for you. Is that OK with you?"

Before I could finish, the glass had fallen from his fingers and broke on the wooden deck. Bob was asleep in the chair.

Between Sandy and me we managed to drag Bob's 235 pound hulk into one of the guest bedrooms. We stripped him down to his boxer shorts and covered him with a light blanket. He was snoring away loudly as we left the room.

****

I followed my wife into the kitchen and sat at the table as she made a pot of coffee.

"Isn't it a little late for coffee?" I asked her.

"We need to talk and I need you awake right now," she said.

She joined me at the table as the coffee brewed and said, "Morgan, you know I love you. You know I find our life together exciting and wonderful. I love the travel and I love being so rich. I love the way you care about people and the way you're always there to help everyone. You're a good, kind, generous man."

She paused and I said, "There's a 'But' in there somewhere."

"But there's going to come a time when our luck is going to run out. You've almost been killed. I've almost been killed. The damn sharks and Cubans almost got us last spring. We can't just continue to race around doing dangerous stuff for everybody in trouble."

"Let me interject a 'But' here, my dear," I said. "Bob and I go back a long way. I don't think I've had a friend as long as Bob has been my friend. And it's just a few phone calls, after all. How do I tell him 'no'?"

Sandy went to the cupboard and took out two large mugs, filled them with the fresh strong coffee and brought them back to the table.

She sipped at the hot brew, her forehead furrowed in deep thought. I was almost done with the mug of coffee I held when she said finally, "I guess you saved my sister. You saved your Cousin Tommy. You saved your friend Lady Jennifer. You caught a killer back in Montana. And you even saved my life when we were stranded at sea. I guess you're just addicted to saving people. How can I ask you to cold turkey now? But promise it will only be a few phone calls."

"That's all he asked for," I said. "That's all I'm going to do."

****

In the morning, before Bob woke up, I made some biscuits, sliced up three really thick ham steaks from a left over shank, brewed a large pot of extra strong coffee, squeezed a dozen big oranges, par-cooked some potatoes and diced them up for home fries.

Sandy sat at the table watching me and said, "I'm sure glad you like to cook."

I grinned and said, "You better go see if Bob is awake. Knowing him, he'll sleep until sunset if we let him."

As I was saying that Bob stumbled into the kitchen, still in his boxers and nothing else, scratching his big beer belly, a cigarette hanging from his pale lips.

"Bob!" Sandy said laughing. "Go put some clothes on . . . and you know there's no smoking in the house."

He took two steps to the sink, ran some water on the cigarette and tossed it into the sink. He started in on his regular morning smoker's hack.

I guess he was either ignoring Sandy's request to put some clothes on or he thought he was dressed. In either case he pulled a chair from the table and sat down.

"Coffee," he said in a raspy growl.

I poured a big mug and set it in front of him. His hands were shaking but he managed to hold the mug with both hands and get it to his lips.

"What the hell did I have to drink last night?" he mumbled.

"Too much wine," Sandy answered.

"Yeah, I guess," he said.

I waited until he had swallowed most of the mug of coffee then asked, "Tell me who you want me to phone."

"Phone?" he questioned. "Phone who?"

"The murders," I said. "You want me to phone and find out why the FBI wants to take over your case."

"Damn! I told you about that? I promised myself I wasn't going to do that," he said.

"Well you did," I said. "So what do you want me to do?"

He hesitated, looked down into his empty mug and then at Sandy who got up and refilled it.

He looked up at me and said, "I really need to know what the hell's going on. I mean, why would the FBI be so interested in the murder of some hookers way out here in San Marcos?"

Despite the fact that Sandy wanted us to get on an airplane and fly as far away as possible, I told my friend Bob Sommers that I would try.

So I scrambled up a dozen eggs and cooked everything else I had prepped. Sandy managed to force some of it into Bob before he went back to the bedroom and got dressed.

He didn't smell very good and he needed a shave, but we sent him on his way feeling secure that he wouldn't drive his beat up old car off the road and down a cliff.

After he was gone and while we were cleaning up the kitchen, Sandy asked, "So who are you going to call?"

"The family sends a lot of money to our Representative in Congress, David Gainesville. I think I'll start with him."

So I phoned him at his office in D.C. and after being shuffled around from clerk to clerk he finally came to the phone.

"Mr. Crew," he said. I could hear the plastic smile on his face. "What can I do for you?"

I explained what was happening in San Marcos, the murders, and the FBI. "I need to know why," I said.

"That's a tough call," Gainesville said. "I'm not sure . . ."

"I really need to know," I said interrupting him. "Make enquiries. And get back to me before you need money for your election campaign," I said and hung up before he could say anything.

****

And so the month of July slipped away and summer wore on into that August day Sandy and I were lounging on our deck, she in the shade, me trying to add to my tan.

We had both let the murders slip from our minds and I gave up waiting for Congressman Gainesville to call me back. Bob never came back to ask how I was doing. I was content to let sleeping dogs lie.

Sandy had suggested we go down to Harborside for dinner and we were discussing which restaurant we would go to when the phone rang. I got up to answer it.

"Morgan," Bob Sommers said. "I gotta see you. Can I come up?"

"We were just on our way out to dinner, Bob," I said.

"I've been fired, Morgan."

THE LINE

Bob arrived at our house less than thirty minutes later. I knew it took at least forty-five minutes to get up the hillside from Downtown. He must have broken every speed limit there was on the way up the hills.

Sandy and I had tossed on a couple of light bathrobes. We sat with Bob in the living room.

"Start at the beginning, Bob," Sandy said.

"I guess I couldn't let go," he began. "I mean, after those two FBI agents told me to quit . . . that was back on July 4th . . . I just couldn't. They took all the evidence, the medical reports, everything. The Medics and the Medical Examiner were threatened. All my cops were ordered to keep their mouths shut.

"But since then," he went on, "There've been two more North Harbor prostitutes murdered. Same M. O., same cuts, same everything. A bunch of FEDs came to town and picked up the bodies and took them away. They threatened everybody. Everybody's scared. I just couldn't walk away," he went on. "I mean, this is my damn town. There's somebody killing people here and I'm just supposed to ignore it? What the hell, huh?"

"You said you've been fired?" I asked.

"Yes," he said. "I've been up to North Harbor asking questions. Sort of on my own . . . Off the clock, you know? I was getting close to a couple of pimps and maybe where the girls worked out of. You know how those people are up there. Nobody talks about anything. But I found a couple of working girls who knew the dead hookers. They were friends apparently. They gave me a couple of names and a couple of bars were the dead girls may have worked . . . You know, where they found Johns.

"Anyway," he said. "I started at the bars but as usual, no one knew anything. I was rummaging around for the pimps, when about two hours ago I got a call from Mayor MacKerney's office. I went to see him right away and he fired me."

"But what did he say?" Sandy asked.

"Not much," Bob answered. "He said something about my being too nosey . . . That I couldn't just let it be . . . That I had to respect authority. He was clearly upset . . . Nervous, you know?"

I didn't know what to say. Bob is my closest friend but what could I do?

"Did you ever make that phone call," he asked me.

"Yes, I did. But I never got a reply."

"OK," he said. "You need to follow up on that. I need something to go on . . . Anything. Get me anything you can."

Sandy nodded silent agreement. She knew that we had to do something for our friend. So I picked up the phone on the table next to me and dialed in Congressman Gainesville's number.

"Hey, Morgan," the Congressman said brightly then just as suddenly his mood changed. "I'm sorry, Morgan. I can't talk to you," he said seriously and in a whisper.

"Wait a minute, Dave. I assume you want to be reelected next year. You know I can make that very difficult for you," I said as firmly as I could manage.

"Look, Morgan," he said in a whispered voice. "Keep out of this, will you?"

I answered as simply as I could when I said, "No!"

"Leave me alone, Morgan. Just leave me alone," he said and hung up the phone.

I turned to Sandy and Bob and said, "This is more than it appears.   The FBI wouldn't be able to threaten a Congressman.   He even doesn't care if he doesn't get reelected, for God's sake."

"OK, then what do I do?" Bob asked.   "I can't just walk away."

"Go home," I said.   "Go home and stay there.   Let me try to find out what's going on."

"No way, Morgan," he said.   "I told you, I'm not just going to go away.   If you're going to do something, then I'm going to be right there with you."

I looked at Sandy and she nodded in agreement.

"OK," I said to Bob.   "In that case tomorrow morning you and I are driving to Sacramento and visit the FBI office there."

"Don't forget me," Sandy said.   "I'm going, too."

"But the MGB only has two seats," I said.

"Then we'll take a car with three seats," she said and stood.   She smiled and walked into the bedroom to dress for dinner.

Bob accompanied us to dinner.   We decided to go to the Country Club because Bob pleaded that we go there.

Mayor MacKerney was there, sitting at a table with two members of the City Council.

We sat at a table on the other side of the dining room and ordered a vodka martini for Sandy and Wild Turkey 101 for Bob and me.   Mayor MacKerney walked to our table as the drinks were set down.

"What's going on here?" he asked.

"I have no idea what you're talking about, Mayor," I said as innocently as I could manage.

"What's he doing here?" he asked looking at Bob.

"He's my guest," I said.

"Damn it, Sommers!   I told you to leave it alone! What the hell do I have to do to convince you!" he yelled too loudly, drawing the attention of everyone in the dining room.

"All I'm doing is having dinner," Bob answered in a quiet voice.

"You've recruited Morgan Crew to help you, haven't you?"

"That's enough, Mayor," I said. "You're making a scene. Everyone's looking at you."

"In my office . . . First thing in the morning . . . All of you. Understand?" he demanded and walked away.

****

First thing in the morning to us meant just after half past ten. We had talked Bob into spending the night at our house. We kept him away from the booze and kept the conversation light. Early to bed – sort of late to rise?

When we walked into the Mayor's office he was there, sitting behind his desk, and the two FBI agents who had ordered Bob off the case were in the two chairs in front of his desk. They stood, the Mayor remained seated.

"I'm Agent Lewis," one of them said. "This is Agent Bradley. Tell me why we should not place the three of you under arrest right now for interfering in a Federal Investigation."

Bob was about to say something but Sandy touched his arm and shook her head.

I took a step forward and said, "I won't give you just one reason why you shouldn't arrest us . . . I'll give you more than a hundred reasons. Harper, Harper, Jascro, and Nettles. They're my attorneys and they love to start their workday by eating guys like you for breakfast. So try me Agent Lewis."

Lewis turned to look at Mayor MacKerney who nodded quietly. Then the Mayor pointed to a few chairs and a leather couch at the side of the room and said, "OK, sit down."

Bob started to move towards the chairs. Sandy again stopped him and shook her head slightly.

I smiled at her, turned to Agent Lewis and said, "No. I think you two should sit down. I have some questions for the two of you . . . And for you Mr. Mayor."

"I ask the questions," Lewis said.

"Later," I said. "Right now, sit down and listen to me."

They hesitated but both men sat and Sandy took Bob to the couch against the wall. I walked to the front of the Mayor's desk and sat on it, facing the two Agents. I pushed the Mayor's name plate and desk set to the side,.

"Let me summarize what I know and you correct me when I'm wrong," I began. "Several prostitutes from North Harbor have been viciously murdered. Murder is a civil crime to be investigated by the civil authorities. Bob Sommers over there is the civil authority here is San Marcos.

"You two Federal Agents," I continued, "come to town unannounced on the Fourth of July and tell him he can't investigate a civil crime. Let us remember that murder without some other Federal crime attached to it is not a Federal crime, and that means you have no jurisdiction here . . . unless there *is* some other Federal crime attached. If there is, tell us now."

They were silent which told me I was right.

"While we're at it," I said. "Let me see your badges and I.D."

Lewis looked at Agent Bradley sitting next to him. Bradley, younger than Lewis and a whole lot tougher looking, said, "I don't need no stinkin' badge . . ."

Both men laughed but they took their leather cased badges and IDs out and handed them to me.

I looked carefully at both. Each had small gold badges and ID cards. I handed them back and said, "So anyway. If there's no federal crime attached, then explain to me . . . And to Bob Sommers . . . Why he shouldn't investigate these crimes."

"Because we said so," Lewis said.

"Not good enough," I said. I pushed myself off of the Mayor's desk and said, "Tell you what I'm going to do. I'm going to stay right at Bob Sommers' side, like we were attached at the hip, and he's going to investigate these murders."

I turned to Mayor MacKerney and said, "And you, Mr. Mayor. You are going to reinstate Bob. You are going to give him all the backing he needs and he will continue as the town's only Detective. Do you agree with that or do I phone my attorneys and have them file suit against the city for unlawful termination of employment?"

Mayor MacKerney said nothing but the two FBI Agents got up, looked around the room at all of us, and walked out.

Sandy whispered to Bob, "See, Morgan can handle it."

Bob stood, walked to the Mayor's desk and MacKerney took Bob's badge and gun from the bottom draw of his desk and handed it to him.

****

Not a word was spoken as we drove away from City Hall in the rented Ford Explorer. I was driving and when I passed by the turn-off that would take us into the hills and back to our house, Sandy said, "Hey. You missed the turn."

"We're not going home right now," I said. "We're going to Sacramento."

"Why?" she asked.

"Those guys aren't FBI Agents," I said. "We need to find out who they are."

"What . . ." Bob said. "But . . ."

"Look," I said. "Do you really think the FBI could be intimidated by me and a bunch of lawyers? Real Agents would have laughed at me and arrested the three of us on the spot. No, those guys were something else . . . but they weren't FBI."

So we drove to Sacramento and found the Federal Building. Inside we made our way to the offices of the FBI and announced ourselves. We had to wait over an hour but eventually the three of were shown into an office where Agent-in-Charge MaryAnne Anderson greeted us.

"Sorry for the delay," she said. "I made a few phone calls and found out who you are, Mr. Crew. What can I do for you?"

I explained in some detail what had happened back in San Marcos, right up to the reinstatement of Bob as Detective Lieutenant.

"So why are you here?" Agent Anderson asked.

"Who are Bradley and Lewis?" I asked.

She paused for a moment then turned to her computer on the side of her desk. She typed in something, then some more. It took a minute but she turned to us and said, "I don't know. They aren't FBI."

It took us the better part of two hours to complete and sign statements. Then we were off, back to San Marcos.

We had missed lunch and late afternoon was giving way to evening. We sat in the kitchen waiting for the two pizzas Bob ordered to be delivered. We were discussing what to do next.

Bob said, "Morgan, Sandy. I really appreciate all you've done for me. But now I need you to step out of this. Leave it to me."

Sandy surprised me when she said, "Bob. Face it, you're a good cop. We all know that. Under ordinary circumstances you would go out there and find the killer and make the arrest and bring him to trial. But these are not ordinary circumstances.

"Morgan," she went on. "Because of his damn family and damn money, can do stuff that you can't do. Would you have your badge back without him? I really think you need to let us help you on this one."

The doorbell rang and Bob paid for the two extra large pizzas with extra cheese and meat he had ordered. He carried them back to the kitchen and laid them on the table.

"Are you really gonna' eat that stuff?" Sandy asked.

"Hey," Bob said. "This is good stuff . . . Great, ya' know?"

"It's nothing but fat and cholesterol," Sandy argued.

"Yeah, delicious ain't it," he said as he tore off a big slice and bit into it.

I took a slice – because I really love that stuff but Sandy would be angry if she knew that. Sandy took a slice, removed the pepperoni, the sausage, the ground beef, and as much of the thick cheese as she could, and then took a delicate bite out of what was left.

I had retrieved beer from the fridge and drank half a bottle before reaching for another slice. Sandy made an angry face that told me it would be the last slice I would enjoy.

Bob finished four more slices and two bottles of beer, sat back seemingly satiated, and said, "OK. You can ride along . . . But I'm in charge, understand?"

In the morning we were off again, doing for a friend what the friend couldn't do for himself, and perhaps putting our own lives at risk. But for the first time in my memory that little voice that lived in the back of my head *wasn't* screaming 'RUN AWAY! RUN AWAY!'

That morning we met Bob at his office Downtown. There was a celebration going on among the small City Police force. They were all happy that Bob was back. Someone had even brought a box of donuts that Sandy wouldn't let me graze at.

Bob waved at us to follow him into his office. We sat

there drinking coffee and watched him eat another donut.

He started, with a mouth full of chocolate iced donut, "I'm gonna' find the pimps. I don't know what you'll do to help, but you're welcome to ride along."

"Is there something else that we can do to help?" I asked.

"Yeah," he said. "There is. Find out who the hell those two guys are."

"And just how do we do that?" Sandy asked.

"Hey," he said, swallowing and smiling. "You were the one said you two could do things I can't. So go do it."

We agreed to at least try and left his office. I drove Sandy and me in the old MGB the two blocks to the City offices and to Mayor MacKerney's office.

"Mr. Mayor," I said as we sat across the desk from him. He didn't look happy but there wasn't much he could do about us being there.

"Talk to me about the two FBI Agents," I said. I wasn't about to tell him we knew they weren't FBI. If he knew that already, I would eventually find that out.

"What do you want to know?" he asked. "They came to town. They said for us to stay out of the case. There's not much more to say."

"What did they say to you? Give me details," I said.

He thought for a minute, leaned back in his tall leather chair, and said, "I did ask them why . . . Why do they want Bob out? They said it was a national security matter. I took their word for it. I don't believe a small city mayor should disregard what the FBI says about national security."

"That's it?" Sandy said. "They say its national security and you fire Bob Sommers? That doesn't make sense. They told you something else."

"Well," he said. "They were very definite that they wanted Sommers out of it. They said it would be on my shoulders if I let him continue. They were very serious."

"And just what were they going to do to you if you

ignored them?" I asked.

"Hey, it's national security. Guantanamo and all that," he said.

"So two FBI Agents are going to pick up an elected mayor of a U. S. city and ship him off to Guantanamo Bay and lock him up with a bunch of terrorists? Is that what you thought?" Sandy said, incredulous at the mayor of her home town.

"Of course," he said. "Hey, it's national security."

There wasn't anything else Mayor MacKerney could tell us. I was sure of that. He had caved at nothing more than me being there. He didn't even ask for a good reason. And he didn't get any of my money for the next election, which he lost by a good margin.

Back at our house I went to the phone and called Congressman David Gainesville's office.

"He's very busy," the woman on the other end of the line said. "Can he get back to you?"

"No, he can't," I said. "He'll talk to me now or find someone else to finance his reelection."

The line went silent for a minute or two, and then Rep. Gainesville came on the line.

"Morgan!" he said brightly. It wasn't Mr. Crew anymore but again I could feel that politically plastic smile of his. "So good to hear from you."

"I suppose it is," I said. "I phoned you a couple of months ago. You never got back to me."

"Oh my God," he said. "You know, you're right. I've been so busy I forgot all about it."

"Well, I can only imagine how busy you've been," I said. "So, anyway. What did you find out?"

"Find out about what?" he asked.

"David," I said seriously. "Don't bullshit me. You know what I'm talking about. Whatever you found out, you were scared to tell me. Or someone told you not to tell me. But you didn't forget to tell me. So tell me now."

There was silence on the line again. Then the Congressman said in almost a whisper, "No, Morgan. Stay out of this."

"Stay out of what?"

"Don't be stupid," he said. I had heard that before and when someone of authority tells me that I shouldn't be stupid, I have always been stupid enough to challenge that authority.

"Screw you," I said. "You tell me or the next phone call I make is to the New York Times. You know how much they love you Republicans."

He was quiet again, and then said, whispering once again, "It's national security. I can't talk to you about it."

"That's the second time I've heard that, Dave. Assume I've got a really big security clearance and tell me what this is all about."

The line went dead. Whatever it was, it was big enough for Gainesville to be scared. He was scared enough not to worry about Crew family money and his reelection.

Sandy and I were eating a couple of sandwiches out on the deck when the front doorbell rang. Sandy went to the door and in short time she was back on the deck with two men.

"Morgan, honey," she said. "Look who's here! These men are from the N.S.A. They want to talk to us."

N.S.A. is the National Security Agency. They are a bunch of spys and spooks who do everything electronically and never talk about it, well, almost never talk about it. So we were getting somewhere. Where we were getting was another question.

"N.S.A," I said. "Terrific. Come on over and sit yourselves down. Want a sandwich? Maybe a Coke?"

"You're thinking this is some kind of joke, Mr. Crew?" the shorter of the two said.

They were certainly official looking, dressed in dark suits, one wearing a starched white shirt and red tie, the other a starched light blue shirt and navy tie. But were they real?

"I'm going to bet it is another joke." I said. "Like those two phony FBI Agents? Now why don't you guys just say what you're going to say, and then head for the door?"

"Get on the phone." The shorter guy said. I guessed he was in charge. "Ask the operator for the phone number of the National Security Agency in Arlington, Virginia. Call that number and when the operator answers, tell her you want to speak with Operation Wolf."

I went into the kitchen, leaving Sandy on the deck with the two . . . guys? After getting the number in Arlington I did as they told me, fully expecting to be the butt of some kind of joke or scam. As it turned out, those two guys were serious; they really were from the N.S.A.

I wasn't told what 'Operation Wolf' was, but it sounded important. A man on the other end of the line wouldn't identify himself, but he said the two men sitting out on the deck with Sandy were for real.

"OK," I said joining them on the deck. "So you really are N.S.A. Now what?"

"You were asked to stay out of the murders," the shorter of the two said.

"Let's start at the beginning," I said. "What are your names?"

They looked at each other, than the talker said, "I'm Mr. Smith. This is Mr. Brown."

"Oh, sure," Sandy said. "How about some I.D., then?"

"We don't carry I.D., Mrs. Crew. Mr. Crew, you know we're for real. Just do what we're asking you to do."

I decided to challenge them a little, if for no other reason than to make myself feel good and also to look like a real man in front of my wife. Like flexing some muscles for her.

"I know a little something about the N.S.A," I said. "You guys deal in electronic intelligence gathering, code breaking, computers, listening in on phone calls, that sort of thing. Why is a spy agency that deals in electronics and computers so interested in the murders of five prostitutes in a little out of the way town like San Marcos?"

"We can't tell you that, Mr. Crew."

I looked at Sandy and then she smiled when the answer came to her.

"You know who killed them," she said knowingly. "You're protecting whoever that is, aren't you? You're protecting a killer who's some kind of spy or something."

"We can't tell you that, Mrs. Crew."

"What can you tell us?" I asked.

"We can tell you to step out of this one, Mr. Crew."

"And what if we don't?" Sandy asked.

"We can't tell you that, Mrs. Crew."

"Doesn't it matter to you folks," I started, "that your guy is out killing people?"

Mr. Brown finally said something, verifying that he could, at least, talk.

"They're just hookers," he said.

"Mr. whatever your name is," Sandy said. "Those women are people. Somewhere they have families . . . Mothers and fathers. Maybe sisters and brothers. They are human beings and they deserve some respect regardless of what they do with their lives."

"Of course," Mr. Smith said. "I'm very sorry. Now just step out of this . . . please."

"What about Bob Sommers," I asked them.

"Lt. Sommers will agree to leave this alone."

They didn't have much else to say and left. But they left without either Sandy or me agreeing to 'step out' as they said.

An hour and a half later we got a phone call from the San Marcos Police Department. Bob Sommers had been shot. He was in critical condition in the I.C.U. of the San Marcos General Hospital.

THE SINKER

Bob had been shot at close range, three times in the back. He had been prowling the dank streets of North Harbor looking for the two pimps he had been told about.

The entire sixteen member San Marcos Police Department were out in force, searching North Harbor for the pimps. They didn't have a name or a description or a place to look. Bob had all that inside his head. But they were making an effort anyway.

The doctors told us that Bob had a badly damaged and punctured lung. A second bullet came dangerously close to his heart, and a third had grazed his spine. That was the dangerous one, we were told. Too much damage there and if he lived he might well be crippled for life. They wouldn't be able to know that for days. He was unconscious and they wanted him to stay that way for awhile.

On the drive back to our house Sandy said, "It's not too late. Let's go to North Harbor."

Over the years I've been with Sandy I learned that it does no good at all to argue with her. She is a strong woman and once she has made up her mind, there was no changing it.

I could tell her it wasn't safe in North Harbor. I could tell her that she could be the next one shot. I could tell her she could be killed. I could tell her she could be kidnapped by space aliens and taken off to planet Xion. It wouldn't make any difference. We were off to North Harbor.

We spent the night making the rounds of the bars and hotels where the prostitutes make a living. Only a few people would even talk to us. Those that did could tell us nothing useful.

I tried buying information – a twenty dollar bill goes a long way in that part of town – but everything we bought turned out to be false leads, North Harbor people just wanting the money.

A little after two AM we decided we'd had enough and started home. As I wound my way through the hills, a thought came to mind. I explained to Sandy, "Look. These murders started back in May or June, something like that. Before then there was nothing. Suppose they started when someone new moved to San Marcos? Suppose the N.S.A. located someone here about the same time? Suppose that person is doing all the killings? Suppose that person who was moved here by the N.S.A. is really important to them?"

"So all we need to do is find out who moved to San Marcos back in May or June? That's brilliant, Morgan. I love you when you're smart."

The next morning we drove into Downtown to the San Marcos Power and Light Company and walked into Jerry Moore's office. Jerry is a senior V.P. there and a long time golfing buddy of mine. He and his wife, Gloria, spend a lot of time at the Country Club. Sandy and I spend a good deal of drinking time with them around the pool.

"Morgan! Sandy!" he said, greeting us. "Good to see you! We haven't seen you at the club for a long time. What's up?"

"Jerry," I began. "I need you to tell me who's new in town. Who started new electric service back in May and June? Permanent residents; not vacationers."

"For anyone else, I'd say no. But for you two . . . No problem. Just don't tell anybody I looked it up for you."

He turned to his computer screen, typed some stuff on the keyboard, and typed some more stuff. Finally his printer started buzzing and spit out a single sheet of paper. He reached over, grabbed it and handed it to me.

There were nine names and addresses on it. We thanked Jerry and promised that we would phone soon to make a dinner date with him and Gloria.

Back in the car Sandy and I read through the list. There were four new residents of North Harbor, one in a Downtown hi-rise condo, two in a nice neighborhood of single family homes just outside of Downtown, one up in the hills just a few blocks from our home, and one in a little valley just over the hills.

The address in the condo was nearest so we started there. The occupant turned out to be a little old lady of about 80 years who was desperate enough for visitors that she insisted we come in for a cup of tea.

Sandy said a couple of minutes wouldn't hurt anything so we each enjoyed a cup of weak tea and a couple of stale packaged cookies.

It was unlikely that the little old lady had anything to do with the N.S.A. so we headed off to a development called Anchor Landing which are nice little single family homes built maybe five or six years ago. Two addresses on the list were there.

There was no one home at the first address we stopped at. The neighbors told us the Fitzgerald family liked to travel. They were gone a lot, they said. Checking calendars with some of the neighbors we found out that the Fitzgerald's had been out of town most of June and all of July. That pretty well eliminated them, we agreed.

The second, just a block away, was the home of a Latino family. The house was immaculately maintained with well placed colorful flowers and trimmed shrubs. The small house had recently been painted in nice, muted colors that fit in well with the neighborhood.

There was Mrs. Ruiz and her five school-age children, her mother and her uncle who looked to be as old as the old lady in the condo. Mr. Ruiz owned a fishing boat. They had lived in San Marcos for twenty six years and had moved from North Harbor after saving money for all those years to buy their dream home.

We agreed the Ruiz family would hold little interest for the N.S.A.

Sandy insisted we go back to North harbor and check out the four addresses there.

"The murders did all happen there, after all," she reasoned. "Chances are whoever killed the girls' lives there, too."

That was logical – of course – so I drove the old MGB back to North Harbor. I felt better about that trip because it was still the middle of the day and the sky was bright blue, the sun lighting up that dangerous place to be.

The first address was a dump of a three story home that had been converted to six apartments. It was probably a nice place maybe 50 years ago. Today it is dark, weather beaten and the bottom of the barrel for the occupants.

The apartment on the list just had to be on the top floor, of course. I was breathing hard by the time we got there.

Sandy said, "I told you to drop those twenty pounds."

I knocked on the beaten up door and then knocked again. The door opened a crack and a foul, stale odor permeated from inside. It seemed to be a combination of old food, body odor, and just plain dirt.

"What'ya wan'?" a raspy voice from inside said through the crack of the open door.

"Just a minute of your time," I said. "Can we come in and talk to you?"

"You cops?" the voice said.

"No . . . we just want to talk to you," Sandy said.

"You a girl?" the voice saked looking with drooping eyes at Sandy.

Sandy smiled at me and said to the voice, "I used to

be a girl . . . I'm a woman now."

The door opened a few inches more and part of a man's face peered out. He looked back and forth at us and then said, "OK. What'ya wan'?"

"Just to talk," I said. "How about twenty bucks to talk to us?"

"Twenty? Nah . . . Ain't 'nuff. It'll cost ya' a hunnert", he said.

We caught a whiff of foul breadth coming from the man. But I agreed to the hundred dollars, pulled a bill from my money clip and handed it to him. He opened the door and we stepped inside the apartment.

It turned out to be one big room, lined wall to wall with metal shelves holding scores of electronics. Computers I recognized but much of the boxes with flashing lights on the shelves were unknown to me.

"Wow!" Sandy said. "You must be some kind of computer wizard."

"I love'em," he said. "You can do anything with computers. You can learn anything."

The man was perhaps 30 years old, but he could have been younger. His clothes were wrinkled and dirty, like he hadn't been out of them for a week or two. His teeth were yellow with a brown cast to them. His hair was long and greasy and dirty and uncombed. His face was cloaked with maybe two weeks stubble.

The room, besides being crowded with electronics, was crowded with old take-out containers of rotting food, empty and half-empty liter bottles of pop, and maybe a half ton of cigarette butts that had been crushed out all over the place.

"What kind of stuff do you learn?" I asked him.

"Why? You think I'm doing something wrong?" he said and stepped back away from us.

"No reason," I said. "I paid you one hundred dollars to talk to you. So I'm talking."

"You're asking, not talking," he said. "And I don't like people stickin' their nose into what I do."

Sandy walked around the cluttered room, looking at all the things that were flashing lights and all the wires going all over the place.

"Let me guess," she said as she looked. "You're a gamer . . . You do some hacking . . . Probably for anybody who will pay you . . . And you download a lot of pornography. How right am I?"

"None of your business," he said. He reached for a keyboard, typed in a few letters and three computer screens went blank very quickly.

"You moved in last May," I said. "Where did you move from?"

"Back east," he said. "Why?

"What brought you to San Marcos?" I asked.

"I rented a truck," he said.

"Not that," I said. "I mean why did you come to San Marcos?

"It's quiet here . . . A small town, ya' know?"

"You can get lost, right?" I asked.

"People'll leave me 'lone. That's all," he said. "That's all. Get out . . . Both of ya'."

I figured we weren't going to get much else out of this very strange person, so we left.

Outside Sandy said, "Well, I think we found our killer."

"Why do you think that?" I asked her.

"Hey, that guy's as weird as they come," she said. "And all that computer stuff? Isn't that what the N.S.A. does? Wouldn't they want a guy like that?"

"You bet," I said. "You're probably right . . . It wouldn't surprise me at all. But let's check out the rest of the list anyway."

The next on our list in North Harbor was another old house converted to small apartments. The apartment we were looking for was – thankfully – on the ground floor.

An old woman, maybe 60 years old but she could have been younger, answered the door. Her hair was grey and uncombed. She wore an old and faded house dress that hung loosely on her. And she was obviously drunk in the middle of the day.

"Wha' the hell you wan'?" she slurred. She had a bent cigarette hanging from her lips and glass of some kind of red wine in her hand.

"Can we talk to you for just a minute or two?" I asked.

"Go 'way . . . leave me 'lone," she slurred and slammed the door in our faces.

"I think we can eliminate her," Sandy said. I agreed and we went looking for the next North Harbor address on the list.

It was above a derelict beer and wine bar. It was the home of a young woman, a prostitute, who by the appearance of her arms was also a drug addict.

"Yeah," she said in answer to Sandy's question. "I knew three of the girls. They were good people and friends of mine."

"Did they work for someone?" I asked.

"You mean did they have a pimp? Everybody down here has somebody . . . A pimp . . . A boyfriend . . . Somebody to pay their bail and help them out of trouble. They worked for Kenney Hollywood. Me too."

"Tell us about Kenny," I asked.

"He's OK, I guess," she said and picked up a cigarette that had been burning in an ashtray. "He's better than some . . . Not so good as others I've known."

"Would he have any reason to kill the girls?" Sandy asked her.

"Why? He drives a big damn red Lexus we paid for. He wears about ten pounds of stupid gold chains we paid for. He drinks expensive liquor we pay for. You think he lives like I do? No . . . he has no reason to kill any of us . . . unless we tried to retire or something"

"Were they trying to retire?" Sandy asked.

"You kidding? And do what?"

I left a hundred dollar bill on a small table near the door as we left. I knew it would probably be spent on drugs but maybe . . . just maybe . . . it would go for some food. I didn't know, but I continue to have hopes for a better world.

On the street I asked Sandy, "Any ideas on how we find Kenny Hollywood?"

"Look for a big red Lexus, I guess," she said and laughed.

The final North Harbor address turned out to be a 1940s single family home. We parked a block away because the street was filled with San Marcos police cars.

Most of the local cops know Sandy and me. A couple of them saw us and walked to us as we approached the yellow tape blocking the sidewalk.

"What's up?" I asked.

"Break-in sometime late last night. The occupants both were shot . . . killed."

"Who were they?" I asked.

"Harry and Martha Schull,' I was told. "Harry got out of Georgia State Prison back in March. Been here since early June."

"What was he in for?" I asked.

"He nearly killed a guy in a store holdup. Shot him. He served 17 years of a 25 year sentence. They should have known better than move here. This isn't any place for anybody to retire to."

It was mid-afternoon and we decided to head home rather than stop somewhere for lunch. Spending a day in North Harbor wasn't exactly the kind of thing that builds up an appetite. So we sat out on the deck, in the shade and ate a few crackers and some good cheese, washed down with a nice cold bottle of California Sauvignon Blanc.

Sandy said, "So far we have two possibilities. The weird guy with all the computers and the dead ex-convict."

"How about Kenny Hollywood?" I asked.

"Honey," she said. "I've learned a few things from you. Motive, means and opportunity. Kenny Hollywood might have the means and opportunity . . . but what motive would he have for killing three of his girls? That's money out of his pocket."

"You're right, of course," I said. "But I don't like pimps anyway. They're no better than blood-sucking cannibals. They live off the flesh and blood of women. I just don't like them."

"And if the killings stop, then it was probably the ex-con and maybe he was killed for revenge," she suggested.

"By Kenny Hollywood?" I said.

"Could be," she answered. "But let's finish the wine and then head off to that address right nearby, OK?"

We agreed and within the hour we were ringing the doorbell on a really nice Dutch Colonial home on the same side of the hill as our home. A man in a stretched out green sweater, wearing glasses and smoking a pipe came to the door. He was maybe 60 years old and sported a beer belly of bragging proportions.

"Yes," he said and smiled. "What can I do for you?"

We introduced ourselves and he said brightly, "Of course. You're neighbors. Of course. Please come in and meet the wife."

Inside we found a comfortable home, like grandparents might have. Lots of reliable but old furniture and photos of family – children and young people – everywhere. And in the living room we were introduced to the man's wife. She sat somewhat slumped in a wheelchair with a vacant stare across a graying face. Her hair was pure white and she looked old beyond her years.

The man introduced her as Mary Robbins. But she didn't know anyone was in the room with her.

"I'm sorry," Mr. Robbins said. "Sometimes she's better than today. Sometimes she can even say hello. But what can I do for you?"

We told him it was nothing. That we had the wrong address, and we left.

"That's too bad," Sandy said. "But it's not too late to go to the address in the valley."

I agreed and drove the old MGB over the winding roads and down into the valley. I took a couple of wrong turns but we managed to find the address on the list.

It was a pretty good size horse ranch, fenced in white, and with a big stone ranch home at the end of a long drive.

At the right of the home was a big red brick horse stable and barn. A youngish woman, perhaps mid-30s, dressed in a tan blouse, jodhpurs and tall riding boots was leading a beautiful horse into the stable. She stopped and turned when she heard our car. We got out and walked toward her.

"I know you," she said. "You're the Crews. We've seen you at the Country Club. Let me put Lady in her stall and we can go to the house."

Inside, her home was very nicely furnished in what appeared to be expensive contemporary, and very homey. There were children's toys spread across the living room floor. The smell of dinner was drifting through the air and it smelled really good, too.

She introduced herself as Mrs. Ian Wainwright. I had heard the name somewhere but that was all. Mrs. Wainwright offered us a drink from a dark wood bar. I took a bourbon; Sandy asked for her usual vodka but this time with tonic rather than have the woman go through all the routine of making a martini.

We sat in comfortable upholstered chairs near a big bay window overlooking a green pasture. "So," she said. "What can I do for you?"

"Well," I started and decided to lie. "You're new to town and the club. We just thought it would be polite to stop by and say hello . . . sort of an unofficial Welcome Wagon type thing."

"How nice," she said. "I do wish I had known you were coming, however. I've been with the horses all day and . . . well you know."

"Not at all," Sandy said. "You look terrific. Very athletic. I've always wanted a horse. Since I was a girl."

"Do you ride?" Mrs. Wainwright asked.

"Not really, but I'd love to try."

"Come by sometime. We can ride together. I have two very gentle mares you'd like," she said smiling broadly.

We sat in silence for a moment or two and then I said, "I really want to apologize. I know you're new to the Club but we've never spoken to you there."

"Oh, don't think twice about it. We love it at the Country Club. Maybe we can get together for dinner there?"

"That's a great idea," I said. "Is your husband here? I'd like to meet him."

"He's out of town," she said. "On business. He works for you, you know."

"He does? I didn't know," I answered.

"Yes, he's an electronic engineer at Bettenger Aerospace."

Sandy turned to me and said, "Don't tell me. You own that, too."

She and Mrs. Wainwright smiled at each other knowingly.

We stayed for about ten more minutes, talking about San Marcos and the Club, and agreed that when her husband returned from his business trip we would meet for dinner.

On the drive back out of the valley Sandy said, "She's a nice lady. We could be friends. How about we buy a couple of horses, Morgan?"

"Sure thing," I said. "As long as you shovel out the barn twice a day, every day."

THE CATCH

Back at our home we were greeted by the little red flashing light on the phone. It was a message from the hospital. Bob Sommers had regained consciousness and he was insisting to speak with us.

I tried not to break all the City's speed laws getting to the hospital. Bob was still in I.C.U. but his eyes were open a crack. We peered at him through the big glass door; he looked terrible, pale and drawn and stuck with tubes and surrounded by machines.

A Doctor approached us and said, "Look, he's not out of danger. He's in bad shape. I have no idea what's keeping him awake but he's fighting the drugs we've been giving him. He's insisting on talking to you but I think that's a bad idea. You can spend a minute with him . . . not more. Let him get out whatever he needs to get out, then go away."

We edged carefully into his room. A nurse was sitting in the corner, flipping through an old edition of some woman's fashion magazine. She nodded to us as we walked to Bob's bedside.

He moved his head slightly to look at us and winced in pain. Sandy took his hand in hers and I said, "Hey Bob. How're you doing?"

Sandy laughed, the nurse laughed and Bob tried to laugh. I never know what to say to sick people and I try to avoid them as often as possible.

Bob whispered something we could not understand.

His voice was weak but there was something he had to tell us. I bent down close to him and heard him say, "Woman . . . Woman."

Bob closed his eyes and his head slumped away from us. There was a faint smile on his pale lips.

Sandy asked, "What did he say?"

"Woman. That's all he said."

"He wants a woman?" Sandy said incredulous.

"I really don't think so," I said. "I think he's trying to tell us a woman shot him."

"A woman! Wow!" Sandy said. "We've been looking under the wrong rocks. We assumed it was a man."

The nurse stood and walked over to us. She glanced at a couple of the monitors and said, "He needs to rest now. You'll have to leave."

Sandy, still holding Bobs hand, said, "Don't worry. We'll find her."

I drove the MGB back up the hills to our home, without coming close to breaking any speed limits. Outside, on the deck, we sat and watched the sun slowly lower itself into the Pacific.

Food wasn't on our minds but Sandy mixed up a shaker of vodka martinis and poured a large Wild Turkey for me.

"A woman," she said sitting next to me. "You still think it's someone new to San Marcos?"

"It almost has to be. The murders started suddenly. I think we have to go on that premise until we find out we're wrong. It's the only lead we have," I said.

"So what have we got?" she questioned. "There's the little old lady in the condo with the tea."

"I doubt it," I said. "Could she attack and cut up five women who are street savvy? And the Ruiz family doesn't seem to fit either. The old lady drunk might be it . . . if she could sober up enough to cut up five women and shoot a gun. Kenny Hollywood's hooker fits."

"How?" Sandy asked. "Why would a prostitute kill five other prostitutes?"

"One," I began. "She's a woman. Two, she might want to eliminate the competition. Three, she might be jealous of all the women Kenny Hollywood has."

"Ok, I can accept that I guess," Sandy said. "But the old lady in the wheel chair . . . I think we can eliminate her."

"Maybe not," I answered. "It could be too convenient."

As I said that the front doorbell rang. I went to the door while Sandy sipped at her second martini on the deck.

Opening the door I saw a bright red Lexus at the curb and a man dressed in an outlandish bright blue shiny silk outfit and a broad brimmed white hat.

"Hi," he said. "I'm Kenny Hollywood and I understand you've been looking for me."

In the back of my mind I had expected Kenny Hollywood to be an overdone movie and TV bad guy; you know, big, black and nasty. Kenny Hollywood was actually pasty white and rather thin. He was shorter than my 6' 2" and hardly a 'bad guy', in spite of his outlandish clothes.

I invited him in and we walked out to the deck where Sandy was waiting.

"Guess what, dear," I said. "Mr. Hollywood has come a'callin'."

Kenny shook his head at the offer of a glass of my Wild Turkey and accepted a martini from Sandy. He sat on the edge of a chaise near us. He sipped at the martini and complemented Sandy.

"Look," he began. "You know my name isn't Kenny Hollywood. I just use that in business."

"Business?" Sandy said.

"Let me start at the beginning," he said. "My name is Kenneth Anderson. I'm a lawyer . . . N.Y.U. Law School, class of '91. I spent a lot of time in New York defending street criminals including a lot of prostitutes. Only a few of them ever paid me.

"My grades weren't good enough to get me into a big firm with a big salary, so I decided to make a new start in California. After an unsuccessful year in L.A. and another in San Francisco, I woke up one morning here in San Marcos. I was broke and hungry so I stopped at the court house and picked up a couple of County cases . . . Hookers again.

"The County paid me a few bucks and on the way out of the Courthouse, one of my . . . clients . . . stopped me on the street. She wanted to know if there was anything I could do to get her pimp away from her. She said he was beating her up a lot.

"I started to walk away but she suggested something interesting to me. She bought me some clothes and taught me how to talk tough. Two days later I was her . . . pimp . . . And a couple of weeks later I had half a dozen women working for me."

"So this other pimp, he just let you take his women away?" I asked.

"No," Kenny said. "I wasn't about to confront them with anything more than some useless legal papers. A couple of the girls knew two guys who were thieves and strong arm types. So I paid them to . . . Convince shall we say . . . These pimps to go away."

Sandy said, "So you went from lawyer to pimp. And I suppose you feed them their drugs, too?"

"These women are going to do drugs regardless of me being there or not. I simply make sure what they buy is safe and won't kill them too quickly. Think what you like," he said. "But I have no reason to kill any of the girls."

"OK," I said. "Let's set aside what we think of you personally. Who do you think killed your . . . women?"

"I don't know," he said. "But I have an idea. There was this guy. Lots of cash, you know? He was going through hookers like you couldn't imagine. Two, sometimes three a night. I waited outside a bar one night and saw him leave with a girl. One of mine. It was dark but I saw enough of him.

"White guy," he said describing the man. "Not too old, maybe 40 tops. Well dressed but not too expensive . . . Off the rack at Nordstrom maybe. Drove a Mercedes SUV. But here's the thing. When he took off a car pulled out from behind and followed. A Toyota, dark color. Followed them to the hotel my girl works in and then left. Two days later the girl was dead. She was the first of five."

"Why were they all working for you?" Sandy asked. "Why not some others?"

"I don't know. I've asked myself that. The only thing I can come up with is all my girls are over 18. I send the young ones home. I won't deal with kids. I don't beat them and I let them keep more money than other guys let them keep. I bail them out and represent them in court for free. Other than that, they're all alike. And they've all been in the business long enough to do anything for money. Maybe there's something there, maybe not.

"All I want you to do is leave me alone," Kenny said. "It's been a couple of weeks and there haven't been any more killings. I'm doing what I can to protect my girls. Just leave me alone."

With that Kenny Hollywood got up and walked out of our house.

"So," Sandy said. "Assuming he's telling the truth, you know what that means?"

"Yes, I do," I said. "I need to make a couple of phone calls."

****

We were followed by two San Marcos police cars as we wound our way slowly through the hills and down into the valley were Mrs. Ian Wainwright was tending to her horses.

She walked out of the stable and stopped when she saw the motorcade. She didn't move as the three cars pulled to a stop in front of her. Sandy and I got out and were followed by four San Marcos uniformed cops. In the driveway, near the house, was a dark color Toyota.

"What happened?" she asked. "Did something happen to Ian?"

"Where is Mr. Wainwright?" I asked.

"My husband?" she said.

"You and Ian are not married," Sandy said. "Where is he?"

As she said this a fourth car, this one a black sedan with darkened windows drove up. A man and a woman got out. Both were dressed in very dark grey and they had very serious looks on their tanned faces.

The woman pulled an ID card from her pocket and held it in front of her for us to see. It said they were from the National Security Agency. They looked real enough. And at that point I really wasn't interested anyway.

"This is now our investigation," she said. "All of you need to leave now."

The four cops looked at me. I said to the Agent, "We're not leaving. You have no jurisdiction to investigate a civil crime."

"This is a national security matter," she said.

"You're talking spies," I said. "You've got to be kidding."

"I'm not kidding. Please leave now," she said firmly.

"No," I said simply and turned to see the woman who we knew as Mrs. Wainwright slowly backing away from us. I called to the four policemen to stop her and hold her.

"Whoever you are," I said to the two Agents. "I fully intend to find out who killed those five girls and shot my friend. You can't stop me from doing that. You have no powers of arrest and you have no authority to stop a civil investigation. You're welcome to stay and listen, but that's all you will do here."

I told the police to serve Mrs. Wainwright with the search warrant for her home and property they had brought with us. Sandy and I, Mrs. Wainwright and the four cops and the two Agents retired to the house. While the cops started their search, I sat Mrs. Wainwright in a chair and stood before her, in the middle of the room full of children's toys.

"Let's start with your name, and remember, I know you're not Mrs. Ian Wainwright."

She paused for a minute and then said, "OK. I'm Nancy Stephens. So what?"

"Why do you claim to be married to Ian?" I asked.

"We've been together for a year. We plan on marrying soon."

"Where is he?" Sandy asked.

"I told you," Nancy said. "He's out of town on business . . . for Bettenger Aerospace."

I told her, "Bettenger Aerospace never heard of him. You're lying again."

She was plainly shocked and surprised. I wondered if she really had believed Ian worked at Bettenger. Was he lying to her all that time?

The two Agents looked at each other, the man shrugged his shoulders and the woman said to us, "He works for us and we want to know where he is."

We were speechless, all of us. To break the silence the Agent said, "He's a crypto-analyst. That's all I can say."

That settled that question. All I needed to know now was who killed the five prostitutes and tried to kill Bob Sommers.

I started, "Tell me about Ian. Tell me about his proclivity for prostitutes."

"I don't know what you're talking about," Nancy said.

Before I could say anything else one of the four policemen came from a back bedroom. He was holding a plastic bag; inside the bag was a 12" butcher's knife that had dried blood all over it.

"That's the knife you used to kill the prostitutes, isn't it?" I asked her.

She didn't answer. She didn't react at all to the question or the knife in the evidence bag. She stared down at her feet.

Sandy then said, "The children's toys. Where are the children?"

"They're in school, of course," Nancy said without looking up.

"It's summer," Sandy said. There isn't any school in session."

"They're out playing, then," Nancy said.

"You have no children, Nancy," Sandy said. "We checked. There's no record of children . . . none of your neighbors have ever seen children. Why all the toys?"

Nancy was getting frightened, that was obvious. She looked up and from person to person surrounding her, and then said, "I wanted children. I always wanted children. We could have had children . . . Ian and me."

"Ian wasn't faithful to you, was he Nancy?" I said.

"I'm a good woman," she said. "I did whatever he wanted to do. All that strange crap he wanted. I was always there for him."

"But he went to prostitutes, didn't he?" Sandy said. "I can understand that, woman to woman, I can understand how you felt. How betrayed you felt."

"You're damn right," she said. "Nothing was ever enough for Ian. I tried, I really did. I wanted to be a good wife . . . I wanted to be a good mother . . . I wanted us to be happy."

"So you had to eliminate the other women," I said. "If they were gone, Ian would come to you, right?"

Nancy turned to Sandy and said, "You understand, don't you? I had to . . . So we could be happy."

"No," Sandy said. "I don't understand killing someone

for any reason. Why not just leave him?"

"I wanted him," she said. "We could've been happy."

"Could've?" I said. "That's past tense. The chance for happiness is all over now? Is that what you're saying?"

She said nothing but I could see a tear try to force its way out of the corner of her eye.

"How about Bob Sommers?" I asked.

She looked down again, her hair falling in front of her face. Then her head rose slowly and I saw someone I hadn't seen before.

Her eyes were on fire; a harsh, dark, evil scowl filled what had been a pretty face. Whoever it was sitting in the chair in front of us bared her teeth and a deep, animal like voice said, "He was too damn close! He was too damn close, the son of a bitch!"

She spat the words out in a voice that couldn't have been that of the sweet, pretty, athletic young woman we had met.

She was handcuffed and led out to one of the police cars. The two Agents followed me out and stood behind me as I peered into the back window, at the woman in the back seat.

"Where's Ian," I asked her.

"You're so God damn smart," she growled. "You find him."

****

It took almost two weeks of searching and digging around the seven acres of land Nancy and Ian had called home. Ian Wainwright's body was found in a shallow grave under a four foot thick pile of horse manure behind the stables.

He had been stabbed multiple times and his throat

had been cut, as had all five of the prostitutes he had been seeing.

Resting on his chest was a revolver that was identified by the crime lab as the gun used to shoot Bob Sommers.

The summer was coming to an end. When Bob was released from the hospital we took him into our home to recuperate. He returned to duty as San Marcos' only detective in early October

The End

AUTUMN KILL

THE HOOK

Sandy and I had flown out to Boston and rented a car there to drive north. Sandy had been hinting about seeing the autumn colors of the northeast. The idea of getting away from my little town – San Marcos – sounded like a good idea after dealing with a bunch of spies and a schizophrenic killer.

In the back of my mind, in day dreams as I was enjoying the last few days of summer, I fantasized about finding a little place back in the deep woods or on some deserted tropical island or on top of some mountain, where people wouldn't be able to come to me asking for help.

Understand this, I like me and I am comfortable with myself. I wouldn't change anything about me . . . except maybe I'd like to drop about 20 pounds or so. And I really don't mind all the wealth I was born into. I like not having to work for a living, although I spend an inordinate amount of my life dealing with the Crew family businesses and investments.

But being the de facto head of the family means that the family, and everyone who calls themselves a family friend, and a whole lot of employees, come to me to solve their problems for them.   Most of the time it's as simple as giving someone some money to help them over a rough patch of life.

Every now and then it's a lot more than that. It means putting my life at risk, and worse yet, it means putting Sandy's life at risk. I just wanted to get away from that.

So a slow drive with the love of my life beside me, keeping off the major highways and stopping often in the painter's palate of the mountains, really took the edge off. I had bought a map at a gas station somewhere but Sandy tossed it out the window as we crossed a bridge over a rushing stream.

"Let's just get lost," she said. "Let's explore and just go where we feel like going."

That sounded like a wonderful idea to me, so we just drove, taking turns that we hoped would go nowhere.

We stopped when we were hungry, at little hamburger stands and wonderful country inns. We took hundreds of photos. We slept in a few cheap roadside motels and a couple really nice places, too.

We had lost track of the days and we had no idea where we were when Sandy shouted, "Stop! Look over there! A real covered bridge! Let's go back and see what's on the other side."

And so for once I had Sandy to blame for what happened next.

****

I managed to turn the car around on the thin two lane road without driving it into a water filled ditch. Sandy wanted to stop in front of the bridge to take a photo. She wanted to stop halfway across to take a photo. She wanted to stop on the other side to take a photo.

Once we had finished taking photos we continued along the road which eventually turned into a pitted graveled surface. But the surrounding hills and fields were beautiful and we went on. The road turned sharply to the left and we saw the little postcard village of West Camden in front of us.

"And where do you think West Camden is?" Sandy asked.

"Hey!" I said. "Don't ask me. You threw the damn map away, remember?"

There wasn't much to the little town. Main Street (and what else would it be called?) was a nicely maintained and well paved roadway with two lanes for traffic and wide enough for curb side parking. It was four blocks long and when it ended the graveled street started again.

Main Street was shaded by manicured trees that had lost almost all their leaves, leaving a carpet of gold and brown on the sidewalks and street. And even in the economy the rest of the Nation was suffering through, there wasn't an empty shop anywhere on Main Street.

We drove slowly taking in the quaint buildings, the antique shops, the little clothing boutiques, a couple of small restaurants, and a lot of smiling people walking up and down the street.

Halfway into town we saw a sign on a street light pole that read, "MARTHA CUNNINGHAM INN". It was mid-afternoon and we agreed we might be far enough into the back country that we wouldn't find any other place to stay that night.

So we turned the corner and there in front of us was a picture perfect country inn. The building was three stories tall and of the American Colonial Period. It looked freshly painted in grey with bright white trim and black shutters. There were flowers everywhere, in gardens in the front and growing up trellises at the side of the front steps and at the corners of the building. A white picket fence surrounded the building and its grounds, and an ivy covered arch opened at the sidewalk to welcome guests.

"Wow!" was all Sandy could say.

"I agree," I said. "I think we can stay here."

"Maybe forever," she said as we parked the car and got out. Inside we were greeted at the front desk by Emma Reynolds who laughed when we asked what State we were in.

"You're in Vermont, of course," she said. Emma was perhaps in her mid-30s. Her hair was thick and brown and hung in gentle waves to her shoulders. She told us that she and her husband David owned and ran the Inn.

After checking in, Emma led us to the second floor and to a big room decorated in Early American grandeur, centered by a big bed with a thick down comforter overflowing the edges of the mattress, and a big, flowery canopy that had those old ideas racing around in my head as soon as I saw it.

Again Sandy could only say, "Wow!"

In answer to my question of who Martha Cunningham was, Emma said, "She's a local hero around here. This is her house. She followed her husband when he joined General Washington's army in 1775. He was killed early in the war. Martha picked up his musket, dressed in his clothes, and fought as a man for almost a year. When she was wounded in a battle down in New Jersey they of course found out she wasn't a man. They sent her home but she wasn't done. She built this house as a hospital and convalescence home for soldiers from Vermont."

"That's amazing," Sandy said. "She was quite a woman, alright. How come she's not in any history books?"

Emma handed us the keys to the room, turned and started to leave. She said as she walked without turning to look at us, "After the war she was hung for murdering her lover. They say her ghost still walks the halls of her house. If you hear anything tonight, don't let it worry you. She hardly ever hurts anyone."

Emma closed the door behind her, leaving us alone and speechless.

"OK," I said. "I vote we don't unpack. I vote we get back in the car and take our chances out in the hills. Hell, they only have bears out there."

"Morgan Crew," Sandy said. "Don't tell me you believe in ghosts!"

"Hell yes!" I said. "Don't you?"

"Of course not," Sandy said. "Emma probably tells that story to everybody who stays here. I'll bet they have to do something to make their guests find their stay interesting. This place is way out of the way. They have to do something to get people to stay here."

"You mean people will stay here just to be scared?" I asked.

"Why do people go on roller coasters?" Sandy asked. "Why do people go skydiving or mountain climbing?"

"So you're telling me we're not going to leave," I said accepting my fate. "And if that ghost gets me during the night . . . It's all your fault, understand?"

****

Dinner was served at half past seven in the Inn's dining room. We weren't sure about the proper dress but since we were way out in the country we decided to meet sort of in the middle and wear semi-casual clothes.

I wore a blue blazer and grey slacks with a pale blue shirt open at the collar. Sandy was magnificent in black slacks and a grey silk blouse.

As it turned out, the other people already seated in the dining room were dressed mainly in blue jeans and plaid woolen shirts. Oh well, we were too hungry to go back and change.

Dinner was country and family style, and consisted of a green salad, a terrific pot roast that was lightly masked in fresh herbs, roasted potatoes and green beans. Sandy and I enjoyed a nice bottle of some kind of red wine I had never heard of but went well with the beef. For desert there was the inevitable something drenched in reduced, thickened and hot Vermont maple syrup. I tasted mine and decided the coffee was better.

After dinner I took note of a small lounge off the dining room where Sandy and I retreated to. Emma's husband stood behind the bar toweling glasses like a good bartender should.

I noticed on a shelf behind him, a bottle of Godet Sélection Spécial V.S.O.P. Cognac! That's something you seldom see in a bar, a really good and almost expensive cognac. So we each had a large snifter of the stuff.

A few of the other people from the dining room filtered in to the lounge; they ordered beers for the most part. Sandy and I were sitting quietly in a corner at a small wooden table. Two of the people, obviously a husband and wife of some years, walked up to us, smiling broadly.

"You must be the folks who just checked in," he said. "We're the Compton's. I'm Eddie and this here is my wife Beatrice."

"Very glad to meet you," I said. "Please sit and join us."

"Why?" Eddie asked. "Are you falling apart?"

Both Eddie and Beatrice laughed at Eddie's 'joke' which is older than I am. But they did sit at the small table with us. They waived to David Reynolds who without asking drew two more beers from the tap at the bar for them.

"So," Beatrice asked. "Where are you folks from?"

"California," I said.

"Up north," Sandy added. "A little town called San Marcos."

"My, that's a long drive," Beatrice said.

"We flew," I said without thinking that the simple statement opened me up for yet another old and tired joke.

I wasn't disappointed when Eddie said, "Did you take a plane or flap your arms really hard?" He and Beatrice laughed again.

Sandy and I stayed at the table long enough to finish our excellent cognac. When our snifters were empty I faked a yawn and Sandy took the hint. She said, "You'll have to excuse us. We're very tired from our drive today. Will we see you at breakfast?"

"Oh, we'll eat at home," Eddie said. "Beatrice is a great cook."

"You're not staying at the Inn then?" I asked.

"Oh no," Beatrice said. "We just came for dinner. As a matter of fact, I think you're the only guests tonight."

"Yeah," Eddie said. "Hope the ghost don't get you!" He and Beatrice laughed once again.

In our room we spent an unusually short time in the shower together. We pulled the down comforter up tight; Sandy switched off the bedside lamp on her side and waited for me to do the same on my side of the big bed.

"You're not planning on leaving that light on all night?" she asked when I didn't reach over to switch it off.

"For a change," I said. "Maybe we could fool around with the light on?"

"Morgan, there is no such things as ghosts. Now turn off the light and go to sleep. Don't make me get up to turn it off," she said.

So, I turned off the light and we both fell asleep almost immediately. The red numbers on the alarm clock on the nightstand read 12:03 AM when the creaking of floor boards woke both of us.

"Sandy, Sandy," I whispered. "Did you hear that?"

"It's an old house, Morgan. Old houses creak. Now go back to sleep."

So I closed my eyes but when the long, slow moan started I opened my eyes and sat up in bed.

"OK," I said.   "Tell me that's just an old house creaking in the wind."

"That is definitely not an old house creaking in the wind," Sandy said.

The moaning continued and got progressively more pain-like. It sounded like whatever was moaning was out in the hallway and coming closer to our room.

"Wait here," I said. "I'm going to find out what the hell that is."

"Not alone, you're not," Sandy said and got out of the bed.

We wrapped bathrobes tightly around us and slowly walked to the door. I put my hand on the doorknob and hesitated. The moaning was loud now and right outside our room.

"Go ahead," Sandy said. "Open it. We've got to know what that is."

So I took a deep breath and pulled at the door as hard as I could. The moaning stopped as soon as the door flung open. The hallway was dark and empty.

We stepped into the hallway. A single small lamp was lit at the top of the stairway. The hallway was cold and silent.

"OK," Sandy said as she grasped my arm. "Maybe you're right. There is something really strange going on here. I think we should pack up and get out of here right now."

"In the morning, Sandy," I said. "Let's try to get some more sleep. We'll leave right after breakfast."

But we didn't get much sleep after that. We both decided to leave our bedside lamps on until the rising sun lit the room.

It was before six AM. We had decided a couple of coffees to go would be enough for breakfast. We had showered and dressed and were packing our bags when we heard the knock on the door.

I called out, "Come in."

The door opened and Sheriff Dan Pickles stepped into the room.

"Mr. and Mrs. Crew," he said. "You're under arrest for the murder of Emma Reynolds."

THE LINE

The West Camden City Jail consisted of two small cells in the back of a Sheriff's office of three rooms on the second floor of the City Court House. I was locked in the cell on the right; Sandy was locked in the cell on the left.

I shared my cell with Benny Newman, the town drunk. He had taken over the cell's only bed. I sat on the floor in a corner. Sandy had her cell all to herself.

It was past eleven before anyone said anything to us. Sheriff Pickles' only deputy walked back to our cells and unlocked each door. The nametag on his uniform said his name was Worthington.

"I have to handcuff both of you," he said. He was a young guy, in his twenties, and sported lots of muscle.

"I have to take you downstairs to court. You're being arraigned today," he said.

"But we haven't even spoken to an attorney yet," Sandy said as she was cuffed behind her back.

"You'll see your attorney downstairs," Deputy Worthington said.

We were ushered into the small courtroom and found its four rows of benches almost full. I recognized Eddie and Beatrice Compton, David Reynolds, and four other people who had been in the dining room the evening before.

Judge Hiram Higgins sat behind his bench which was

raised above the courthouse floor a foot or so. He was grey haired and looked old. His jowls sagged and his nose was red. He wore thick glasses that rode cautiously at the very tip of his nose.

"Are we ready yet, George . . . I mean Mr. Prosecutor?" he said in a deep, phlegm filled voice.

George, sitting at a small table, stood and said, "Yes, Your Honor. The City versus Morgan and Sandy Crew is ready."

The Deputy removed our handcuffs and indicated that we should sit at another small table next to the Prosecution's. We sat but almost immediately Judge Higgins said, "Morgan and Sandy Crew. Please stand."

We stood. This was becoming all very confusing for the two of us. Not only had we been arrested for murdering the young lady who ran the Inn, now we were in front of a Judge just hours after being arrested. We had not been allowed to phone an attorney and I guessed we weren't going to get one in court either.

"Your Honor," I said. "Can you please tell us what the hell is going on here?"

"You watch your tongue young man," Judge Higgins said, wagging a bent finger at me. "This is a good Christian community and I'll have no hells and damnation in my courtroom."

"I'm sorry Your Honor. But I don't understand. Are we being charged with murder?"

"You have been charged, young man," he answered. "You are now being arraigned before your trial tomorrow morning."

"But we don't even have an attorney, Your Honor," I argued.

"What!" The judge said, but I figured at the time that he may have been feigning surprise.

"Deputy Worthington," the Judge said. "Go get Billy Willey and tell him to get here fast. In the mean time . . .

you two," he said to Sandy and me. "Sit down and shut up."

We sat but I thought I would risk whispering to Sandy.

"Are you as confused as I am?" I asked her.

She whispered back, leaning slightly towards me. "More. I have a hunch we're in real trouble here. These people are really backwoods types. Do you think they plan to eat us for dinner?"

I looked at her and said, "What do you think was in that pot roast last night? The people who checked in the day before us?"

"Stop making jokes," Sandy said. "This is serious."

The judge slammed his gavel down on his bench four times and shouted, "I thought I told you two to shut up! Any more from you and I'll have you chained and gagged."

So we sat in silence for twenty five minutes until Billy Willey walked into the courtroom. Our defense attorney may well have fought in the Revolution with Martha Cunningham and her husband. He walked with a cane and shuffled down between the public benches to our table.

He said without looking up at the Judge, "OK, Hiram. I'm here now. Let's get on with it."

"Alright, George," Judge Hiram said. "What are the charges?"

Our lawyer, Old Billy as I got used to referring to him, tried to push himself out of the chair, unsuccessfully, and said, "Defense waives a reading of the charges, Hiram."

"In court you call me Judge, you got that Billy?"

"Oh sure . . . Your Honor. I just forgot," Old Billy said.

I jumped up and said, "Wait a minute. I want the charges read. I don't even know what the hell I'm charged with."

"What did I tell you about that dirty mouth of yours, young man?" the judge said as he slammed his gavel down five or six times. "I'm not going to warn you again. You are charged with murder . . . that's all you need to know."

The Judge sat back in his tall chair and turned to

George.

"Alright George, present your first witness before I hold these two young people over for trial."

George called David Reynolds to the stand.

"OK, David, we all know you, but for the record tell us your name," George said.

"David Reynolds . . . widower of the fine woman those two over there killed."

I turned to Old Billy but he seemed to be dozing off. I elbowed him and he turned to me and said, "Ssshhhh."

"Tell us what happened, David," George said.

"As soon as they checked in that guy there was after Emma. He tried grabbing her as soon as she stepped around the front desk. He wouldn't let her out of the room and the woman was helping him."

"How do you know that?" George asked.

"Emma told me. She was real upset."

George seemed to be waiting for David to say something else. When he didn't, George asked, "David . . . Did anything else happen?"

"Oh yeah," David said finally. "In the lounge that guy made another pass at Emma. He got rough with her."

"You saw this?" George asked.

"Yeah, I was there alright. And so was Eddie and Beatrice, and Frank and Mabel, and Evan and Marie. They all saw it."

"That's it, Your Honor," George said. "That's my prima facia case against these two."

Judge Hiram then said, "Eddie, Beatrice, Frank, Mabel, Evan and Marie. You stand up right now."

They did, in unison. Judge Hiram asked, "Did each and every one of you see what happened in the lounge as described by David Reynolds?"

They said, in unison, "Yes Your Honor."

"OK, sit down. George, do you have anything else?"

"Yes Your Honor," George said. "Sheriff Pickles

found this knife at the Inn," he said holding up a wooden handled steak knife. "It was the knife used to kill Emma and it has Mrs. Crew's finger prints on it."

"Of course it does!" Sandy shouted. "That's the knife I used for dinner last night. And where's all the blood that should be on it? And your finger prints are all over it, too!"

"That will be enough of that, young lady," Judge Hiram said. "Let your attorney speak for you."

"He's asleep!" Sandy shouted.

Hiram ignored that fact and said to George the Prosecutor, "Anything else, George?"

"That's about it, Your Honor," George said and sat down.

He turned to us and said, "Do you have anything to add to this?"

Old Billy was snoring. I poked him a little harder this time and said, "Aren't you going to say anything? Aren't you going to examine the witnesses? They're all lying!"

He leaned close to me and said, "Ssshhhhh," again.

"Nothing to add at this time, Hiram . . . I mean Your Honor. Bail requested," Old Billy said without getting up.

"Any objection, George?" the Judge asked.

"No objection if the amount is big enough to guarantee they'll show up for trial."

"Morgan and Sandy Crew," the Judge said. "Stand up."

We stood, Old Billy started to snore again.

"I know who you are. I know all about you. You think being rich allows you to do anything. You think you can kill one of our beloved citizens . . ."

"We didn't kill anyone, Judge," Sandy interrupted.

"Young lady," he said sternly. "I'm going to let you get away with that interruption because I only had to warn you once and I like to give second chances to pretty women. But don't do it again."

A strained look of deep thought and consideration

came across his face. It stayed for maybe half a minute and then he said, "Two million dollars bail," and slammed his gavel down once very hard.

Sandy grabbed my arm before I could say anything and whispered to me, "We have to get away from here. Pay them the two million, let's get in the car and get as far away as possible. After we're safe we can call in the State authorities."

"I'm going to pay," I whispered back. "But I'm not going to leave. This is a sucker's operation and I'm going to put an end to it."

I said to Judge Hiram, "Your Sheriff has my checkbook. Let me have it and I'll write a check."

****

It took a couple of hours but we were finally released with all our belongings. As we walked out the front doors of the Courthouse we were met by Old Billy on the sidewalk.

"Look," he said. "The best thing you can do is get in that car and leave town. Forget this whole thing."

"Are you kidding?" I said. "And have a felony murder warrant on our asses? We wouldn't make it out of State."

Old Billy said, "I think I can talk Hiram into dropping this whole thing in exchange for the two million bail you put up."

"Yeah," Sandy said. "I kind of figured that out already. This is a really good scam you folks have going here, isn't it? You support the whole town running this trick over and over again with every sucker who stops overnight, don't you?"

"I don't know what you're talking about," he said.

"Do we look that stupid?" I said. "Look at this town. It's picture perfect. There's a lot of money floating around here yet it's like fifty miles from the highway. How do you do it?"

"We have a really big cheese industry here, Mr. Crew. The City owns it. We ship out tons of the stuff. The profits are divided up between everyone here."

"Bullshit!" I said. "Your whole town is running this scam and I'm going to put a stop to it."

"Be careful what you say . . . and do, Mr. Crew. There are good people here and they don't like to be talked about like that."

"So where's Emma?" Sandy asked. "I'd like you and me to go see the body."

"Too late," Old Billy said. "The body has been cremated according to her written wishes."

"Oh right! Of course!" I said. "And if we look around town we won't see Emma buying new shoes somewhere, will we?"

"My best legal advice to you, Mr. and Mrs. Crew, is to get in your car and get out of town," Old Billy said, turned and walked away with the assistance of his cane.

****

It was a short two blocks back to the Inn. David Reynolds was at the front desk. He glared at us as we walked in but said nothing.

We started up the stairs and he stopped us.

"Where the hell are you going?" he snarled.

"Up to our room," Sandy said.

"You don't have a room here. Your bags are down here. Get out," he said.

"Where do we sleep then?" I asked. "We have a trial to attend in the morning."

That seemed to stump David. After thinking for awhile he asked, "You're not leaving? I thought you'd leave."

"No," Sandy said smiling nicely. "We're going to stay for the trial. Surprise, surprise."

As we reached the top of the stairs we saw David reaching for the phone. I guess their little scam was falling apart and he was scared.

We ate dinner in a little coffee shop a block away because David said we weren't welcome in the dining room, even though we would have been his only customers. We ordered ham and cheese sandwiches, coffee and apple pie. It was good but we were charged $200 by the waitress who had a hulk of a retired Marine who was the cook standing behind her to make sure the bill was paid and a hefty tip was left.

Back in our room the creaking floors and ghostly moaning went on all night. About midnight I took Sandy by the hand and walked into the hallway. The creepy noises didn't stop this time.

I had a small flashlight and pointed it at the hallway ceiling. I pointed out to Sandy that there were a series of small speakers.

"There's our ghosts," I said.

****

We woke up early, before the sun was up. We lay in bed talking, trying to decide what we would or could do that day.

We agreed that we had thrown a monkey wrench into the works when we refused to leave town. My guess was, and Sandy agreed, that we were the first to not cooperate. The City of West Camden had become used to running this scam; we agreed to that also. And we agreed that we had no idea what would happen to us next.

As the sun began to light the sky we showered and dressed and cautiously walked down the staircase. David was not at the desk. David was not in the dining room. David was not in the kitchen. In fact, no one was anywhere inside the Inn.

So, between the two of us we whipped up a little breakfast and too much coffee. Sandy found some table clothes and silverware and set a table for us. Just for the heck of it, I stepped outside onto the front porch to look for a newspaper. There were none there and looking up and down Main Street, I could not see any newspaper boxes at all.

After eating we walked back to the Courthouse. The front doors were standing open so we walked in. The silence inside was deafening. Inside the Courtroom was like a cold cave, empty and dark.

I found a board on the wall near the building entrance that listed different offices in the Courthouse. The City Attorney's office was near the courtroom. We went there and found no one. In fact, the entire three story building was completely empty.

We stood outside on the steps and wondered what to do next. The sun was shining brightly in a clear sky but the autumn air had a bite to it. Main Street was what artists look for; color everywhere and the buildings straight out of a Normal Rockwell painting.

We walked all four blocks, first on one side of the street, and back again on the other side. Not one shop or business was open; the whole town was devoid of people.

Sandy held my hand and said, "What do you think? The Twilight Zone maybe?"

"I think they're trying to scare us again, my dear," I said. "The ghosts weren't enough and the murder accusations weren't enough. I think this is just something else these people dreamed up."

"So what do we do?" she asked.

"I think we get in the car, drive a couple of miles out of town, and then come back and see if the good citizens of West Camden have materialized."

Which is exactly what we did. Five miles past the City's boundary I spun the car around and sped back to West Camden. Sure enough, Main Street was alive with people but as they saw us coming it was as if a sudden arctic freeze had settled over the town.

I pulled to a stop at the curb in front of the Courthouse and we waited. The two or three minutes that went by seemed like a lifetime but finally Sheriff Pickle walked out the big double doors of the Courthouse.

"What the hell are you doing?" he said. He seemed truly confused at us being there.

"Why Sheriff," Sandy said. "We didn't want to miss our trial."

"Do you really know what you're doing?" he asked.

We just smiled at him. He said, "OK. Go back to the Inn. I'll tell you when your trial will begin."

I parked the car in front of The Martha Cunningham and rather than do what the Sheriff told us to do, we decided to walk up and down Main Street again. As we walked we smiled and said hello to the citizens of the quaint little town. They just starred at us. A few doors were locked as we approached. They just didn't know how to handle us, I guess.

As the hours passed by we started to get tired of walking and we were getting hungry for lunch.

"What say?" I asked Sandy. "Another two hundred dollar sandwich or back to the Inn?'

"I say the Inn," she said. "We can raid the kitchen again because I doubt David will be there."

"Great idea," I said and we quickened our pace back to the Inn.

As we suspected, David was not at the Inn, no one was there. We found sandwich makings – several packages

of sliced meats and of course a lot of Vermont cheddar –
and sat at our breakfast table. I had found several bottles of
red wine I had never heard of before and opened one which
perhaps would have been better left corked.

As we ate, a woman walked into the dining room and
sat, uninvited, at our table.

"Hello," she said, her elbows on the table and leaning
towards us. "I'm Kitty Hanks. I'm the Mayor of West
Camden. I should say, the newly elected Mayor. I was late
for the City Council meeting and when I arrived I found they
had elected me. Oh well."

Sandy was the first to speak, I assumed trying to keep
me from shouting and threatening the Mayor.

"Very glad to meet you, Mayor," she said. "But why
are you here?"

"I'm here to apologize to you," she said. "This whole
thing has gotten out of hand. It's all because we're a very
small town and we have no experience in murders. There
hasn't been a murder here in my lifetime and I was born
here. Sheriff Pickles didn't act professionally and I've
already reprimanded him for the way he handled this. And
I've talked with all his witnesses. Sheriff Pickles influenced
them to lie in court."

She paused, still smiling, and looked back and for
from me to Sandy and back to me, waiting for us to say
something.

When neither of us said anything she said, "I have
your check here."

She reached into her purse and pulled my two million
dollar check out, laying it on the table in front of us.

We didn't touch the check nor did we say anything.

"I hope you'll accept my apology," the Mayor said.

I looked at Sandy and she nodded slightly, telling me I
should go ahead and let loose.

"Mayor Hanks," I began. "I would say 'with all due
respect' except I have no respect for you or your town. You

folks are running a scam here. You are way off the beaten path. Only a few people ever find your little village and those people for the most part have some money. They drive into your trap; you scare them with ghost stories and then accuse them of a crime.   You collect bail from them and then encourage them to leave town. Most are probably scared of spending another night here with the ghosts.

"The mistake you made with us," I went on, "is that you got greedy. You had done background checks on us and found out we had a lot of money. You thought you could get a couple of million from us. But we didn't leave town. We stayed and we're going to go on staying until we break up this whole damn scam and your whole damn town."

Mayor Kitty Hanks said nothing.   The smile disappeared from her face. She pushed herself away from the table and she walked away.

"OK," Sandy said. "What do we do now?"

"I'm really not sure," I said. "Maybe there's someone in town who we can flip. Maybe we should contact the State Police or the Governor. I'm not sure."

We agreed that we would start walking the four blocks of Main Street and talk to anyone who would talk to us. So we finished lunch and left most of the no-so-good wine on the table, pocketed the two million dollar check, and walked out of the Inn.

In two hours of walking back and forth, up and down the four blocks of Main Street, no one would talk to us. There was an ice cream shop that we passed several times, and about three that afternoon we decided that we were due a break.

Inside we found something out of the 1890's; a marble toped counter with tall stools lined up in front of it. There were big glass jars filled with candy and a sign above reading "PENNY CANDY". There were four hand pumps that dispensed sodas and seltzers.   Six small tables centered the room; each had a couple of filigreed metal chairs. And the whole place was done in pink and white stripes.

Sandy said as we stood in the doorway, "Disneyland."

We sat at the counter and waited for the waitress behind the counter to take our orders. There was only one other couple, teenagers sharing a glass of root beer at a table. And we sat . . . and we sat . . . and the waitress never came close to us nor did she even look at us.

Finally I said, "Excuse me. Can we get something to drink?"

She went out of her way to ignore us. We waited a few more minutes then got up and left.

Out in the street Sandy said, "I think we're wasting our time out here. The only place we're going to get anything to eat is back at the Inn."

In the kitchen at the Inn we found five bottles of cold Coca Cola. We leaned against a stainless steel table, both of us wondering what we would do next . . . If there was anything we could do.

From behind us we heard a sound, a door creaking and soft footfalls. We turned and saw Emma Reynolds standing there.

She wasn't a ghost but she looked pretty bad. Besides her hair being disheveled and in knots, her left eye was swollen shut. That side of her face was the most amazing mix of blue and black and purple and even some green. Her bottom lip was swollen and cut badly. Her dress was torn and her knees were cut and bloody.

"What happened to you?" Sandy said as she went to her. She tried to take Emma into her arms but the woman stepped back away from Sandy. She had been crying and started crying once again.

In a weak, sobbing voice Emma said, "I'll help you if you get me out of this place."

THE SINKER

The three of us sat at a table in the dining room. Sandy had found some tea bags in the kitchen and had boiled some water. Emma sipped at the hot mug of strong tea Sandy had placed on the table in front of her.

"What happened to you?" I asked her.

"David and Sheriff Pickles." She said.

"David?" Sandy said surprised to hear that. "Your husband did this?"

"He's not my husband," Emma said. "That's just part of the game."

"The game?" I said.

"You have to promise me that you'll take me with you," Emma said.

"You have my word that you'll go with us. Just cooperate . . . Tell us what this is all about," I said.

Emma told us much of what we already knew; that the town of West Camden was in the business of blackmailing the people who found their way into town. It had been going on for years.

"But never like what they're doing to you," Emma said. "They've never used murder before but they got greedy and wanted your money."

"You said David isn't your husband," Sandy said.

"That's right," Emma said. "This whole town is a lie. Nothing's real. Whatever money they get from people like you goes first to keep the town looking good. The rest is divided equally among the people."

"How much does the town take in, Emma?" Sandy asked.

"It's been a lot.   Hundreds of thousands a year, I guess. I never liked what was going on," she said. "But I always thought it was a harmless crime. I mean the people who come to town have the money to spare. And they've never asked for more than the people have. They do really extensive backgrounds on everybody. But they've gone too far with you. I just can't take it anymore.

"I told them I didn't want to do this anymore," she went on, "I didn't think it was right; my conscience was bothering me about the whole thing. Sheriff Pickles and David beat me up. I lied to them; I told them I would go along with it just to get them to stop."

"Are you willing to testify in court?" I asked her.

"If you get me away from here . . . Yes."

We quickly packed our bags and the three of us went to our car in front of the Inn. Emma huddled down in the back seat, Sandy and I in the front.

I turned the key . . . nothing. I tried again and still not a sound from the engine.

Sandy said, "Look under the hood?"

"Sure," I said. "Just tell me where the engine is. I've never changed a damn spark plug. There's always been enough mechanics around to take care of that stuff."

Emma stayed crouched down in the back when Sandy and I got out. Mayor Kitty Hanks was walking slowly towards us. She was smiling like she was very satisfied.

She stood in front of us and said, "I asked you to leave. I apologized and even gave you your money back."

Mayor Hanks looked back and forth from Sandy to me then looked at Emma in the back of the car. She said, "Now you can't leave."

She stepped around us and walked away. Across the street Sheriff Pickles stood looking at us.

"I think we're in trouble," Sandy said.

"I think you're right," I answered.   "Let's get back inside. At least until we figure out what to do."

Emma followed us back into the Inn. She was crying again.

As we stepped inside we were met by a dozen or so town's people carrying out all the food and drink from the kitchen. They said nothing as they passed us; their eyes were lowered so they wouldn't have to look at us. When they were done there wasn't one scrap of food, drop of wine, ounce of liquor, or bottle of soft drink left at the Inn.

Sandy asked Emma, "Is there a way out of town? Can we get a car anywhere?"

She thought for a moment and then said, "There are lots of cars. Getting one might be difficult. I'm scared of them. I think they'll stop us."

"If we try early in the morning," I said.   "Before anybody's awake, maybe we can find a car and be gone before anyone knows. Until then, I suggest we stay here. The streets might not be safe."

We retreated to our room, Emma staying very close to us. She was tired, exhausted. She lay down on the bed and was asleep almost immediately.

Sandy put a finger to her lips and motioned silently to me to leave the room. In the hall she said, "Let her sleep. We need to talk."

I used our room key to lock the door and we wound up downstairs in the dining room, sitting at our still set table.

"Can you hotwire a car?" Sandy asked.

"Hotwire?" I asked.   "Hell, I can barely get the damn key into the ignition of my own MGB."

"We might have some trouble getting a car," Sandy explained.   "Unless these people leave their keys in their unlocked cars."

"I wonder if Emma has a car." I said.

Before Sandy could answer, three shots rang out in

the empty Inn. We were frozen for a second or two, and then we jumped up and ran up the stairs to the bedroom where we had left Emma. The room's door, that I had locked, was standing open. Inside Emma lay on the bed in a pool of blood.

From behind us Sheriff Pickles said, "OK, hands up. Don't try anything or I'll shoot you."

We were handcuffed and taken back to the City Jail. This time we shared the cell on the right. We were left alone in the cell, still handcuffed, for about a half an hour.

We stood as a group of people walked into the Sheriff's office. In the lead was Mayor Hanks. Sheriff Pickles stood at her side. Deputy Worthington was in the small crowd. I had seen a few of the people behind the out on Main Street. They stood on the other side of the bars.

Mayor Hanks spoke to us. "Now you *have* committed a murder. Now it won't be possible for you to buy your way out. Now you're going to prison for the rest of your life."

"That was bail," I said. "We weren't buying our way out of anything. We stayed for our trial. The court record will show that. It will also show how ridiculous that comedy of a hearing was."

"I assure you," the Mayor said. "The record of your hearing will reflect that everything was done to protect your rights against the charge of the murder that occurred this evening."

"But . . ." Sandy started and was interrupted by Mayor Hanks.

"But nothing. It's your word against every person in West Camden. You had your chance. Just one word of advice . . . Don't try to escape. Our Sheriff is a very good shot."

THE CATCH

And so we waited. They didn't remove the handcuffs from either of us which made getting any sleep impossible, plus there was only one steel bunk with a thin mattress in the cell. We sat on the bunk, next to each other and tried not to show each other how frightened we were.

I couldn't tell the time of night but the sky outside was just beginning to show the faintest sign of the sun rising. I heard the door to the Sheriff's office squeak open and saw Sheriff Pickles walk into the jail.

"Stand up," he commanded. "Over here and backs to me. I'm going to take your cuffs off."

Without argument we did as he told us to do. He then unlocked the cell door and swung it open.

Come on out," he said. Again we did as he said.

"Where are we going?" Sandy asked.

"Shut up! Outside," he said pointing at the front door.

Outside on the street Sheriff Pickles opened the door of his big Ford pickup.

"Get in," he said.

"Where are we going?" Sandy asked again.

"Shut up and get in," he said.

Looking back on it, I probably should have tackled the Sheriff right then and there. Between Sandy and me we probably could have taken him and drove off in his marked police pickup. But we got in the front seat instead.

Sheriff Pickles drove out of town in the opposite

direction we had arrived from. The road was narrow and winding. The trees were all beautifully colored and a little stream ran alongside the road.

He pulled the truck to the side of the road and stopped. He pulled his pistol from its holster and told us, "Get out."

He motioned for us to step across the small stream and walk into the field on the other side. In the field we saw two fresh mounds of dirt at the sides of two holes big enough to be graves.

"Oh my God!" Sandy screamed. "He's going to kill us!"

There was a grove of evergreen trees off to our left. From it Deputy Sheriff Thomas Worthington stepped into the field. He held a semi-auto pistol, pointed directly at Sheriff Pickles.

"I can't let you do this Dan," he said. "I can't let you kill anybody else. I didn't sign up for this."

"Come on, Tom," the Sheriff said. "You know we have to do this. These people can ruin everything. You don't want that, do you?"

"I don't want any more killing," Deputy Tom said. "You killed Emma. You shouldn't have done that. I'm not going to let you kill anyone else."

The Sheriff moved suddenly and quickly. He managed to fire one shot at his Deputy before Deputy Tom filled his chest with four bullets.

Sheriff Pickles lay dead in the wet grass of the field. Tom Worthington had been hit in the right shoulder. He was bleeding badly but he could stand and talk to us.

"I'm going to get you out of here," he said. "You'll have to drive. My car is around the bend."

Tom told us to continue along the road away from West Camden. He said we needed to drive about 20 miles to a highway and head north. We would find a State Police Office.

We found it and Tom was given the medical attention he needed. Eight days later Sandy and I were on a jet, flying back home.

The quaint and pretty little Town of West Camden was raided and occupied by the Vermont State Police and the State's Attorney General's office. Massive arrests were made.

It took a very long time . . . years in fact . . . but Mayor Kitty Hanks, David Reynolds, the entire Town Council and a couple of other prominent citizens were convicted of conspiracy in Emma's murder. By court order, almost the entire town and everything in it was sold off to pay fines and legal costs and to at least partially reimburse those who suffered by accidentally finding West Camden.

My advice: Be careful where you drive to.

The End

www.ingramcontent.com/pod-product-compliance
Lightning Source LLC
Chambersburg PA
CBHW020246150626
46552CB00020B/608